"You're going hom

"No—"

"Don't argue with me. Y[...] killed. No telling what [...] happened to Simon." He reached out and laid a palm against Simon's cheek. "The baby needs a safe place for a while. And I want some answers."

"Thanks for rescuing us, Cain, but I can't stay with you." Alanna gathered all her strength to remain still when he tried to urge her forward. "Please, just let me go."

"I'm not letting you drive off tonight with Simon. And if you don't level with me about my brother, I'll haul you in for withholding information in a murder investigation."

"Please, Cain, no."

His steely gaze didn't waver. "If you don't want me to call the police in, you have to tell me what's going on."

Alanna reached for the car door handle. Cain grabbed it first, wrapping one arm around her. "Don't get any ideas about running. I'm going to be right behind you."

Dear Harlequin Intrigue Reader,

Spring is in the air…and so is mystery. And just as always, Harlequin Intrigue has a spectacular lineup of breathtaking romantic suspense for you to enjoy.

Continuing her oh-so-sexy HEROES INC. trilogy, Susan Kearney brings us *Defending the Heiress*—which should say it all. As if anyone *wouldn't* want to be personally protected by a hunk!

Veteran Harlequin Intrigue author Caroline Burnes has crafted a super Southern gothic miniseries. THE LEGEND OF BLACKTHORN has everything—skeletons in the closet, a cast of unique characters and even a handsome masked phantom who rides a black stallion. And can he kiss! *Rider in the Mist* is the first of two classic tales.

The Cradle Mission by Rita Herron is another installment in her NIGHTHAWK ISLAND series. This time a cop has to protect his dead brother's baby and the beautiful woman left to care for the child. But why is someone dead set on rocking the cradle…?

Finally, Sylvie Kurtz leads us down into one woman's horror—so deep, she's all but unreachable…until she meets and trusts one man to lead her out of the darkness in *Under Lock and Key*.

We hope you savor all four titles and return again next month for more exciting stories.

Sincerely,

Denise O'Sullivan
Senior Editor
Harlequin Intrigue

THE CRADLE MISSION
RITA HERRON

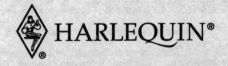

TORONTO • NEW YORK • LONDON
AMSTERDAM • PARIS • SYDNEY • HAMBURG
STOCKHOLM • ATHENS • TOKYO • MILAN • MADRID
PRAGUE • WARSAW • BUDAPEST • AUCKLAND

ISBN 0-373-22710-8

THE CRADLE MISSION

Copyright © 2003 by Rita B. Herron

All rights reserved. Except for use in any review, the reproduction or utilization of this work in whole or in part in any form by any electronic, mechanical or other means, now known or hereafter invented, including xerography, photocopying and recording, or in any information storage or retrieval system, is forbidden without the written permission of the publisher, Harlequin Enterprises Limited, 225 Duncan Mill Road, Don Mills, Ontario, Canada M3B 3K9.

All characters in this book have no existence outside the imagination of the author and have no relation whatsoever to anyone bearing the same name or names. They are not even distantly inspired by any individual known or unknown to the author, and all incidents are pure invention.

This edition published by arrangement with Harlequin Books S.A.

® and TM are trademarks of the publisher. Trademarks indicated with ® are registered in the United States Patent and Trademark Office, the Canadian Trade Marks Office and in other countries.

Visit us at www.eHarlequin.com

Printed in U.S.A.

ABOUT THE AUTHOR

Award-winning author Rita Herron wrote her first book when she was twelve, but didn't think real people grew up to be writers. Now she writes so she doesn't have to get a *real* job. A former kindergarten teacher and workshop leader, she traded her storytelling for kids for romance, and writes romantic comedies and romantic suspense. She lives in Georgia with her own romance hero and three kids. She loves to hear from readers, so please write her at P.O. Box 921225, Norcross, GA 30092-1225, or visit her Web site at www.ritaherron.com.

Books by Rita Herron

HARLEQUIN INTRIGUE

486—SEND ME A HERO
523—HER EYEWITNESS
556—FORGOTTEN LULLABY
601—SAVING HIS SON
660—SILENT SURRENDER†
689—MEMORIES OF MEGAN†
710—THE CRADLE MISSION†

HARLEQUIN AMERICAN ROMANCE

820—HIS-AND-HERS TWINS
859—HAVE GOWN, NEED GROOM*
872—HAVE BABY, NEED BEAU*
883—HAVE HUSBAND, NEED HONEYMOON*
944—THE RANCHER WORE SUITS

*The Hartwell Hope Chests
†Nighthawk Island

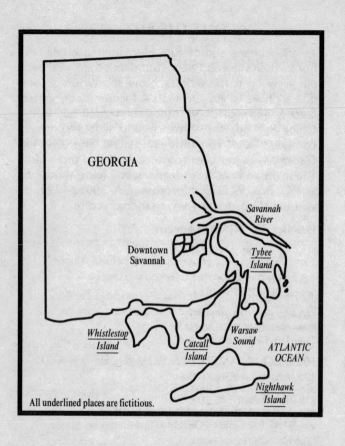

GEORGIA

Savannah River

Downtown Savannah

Tybee Island

Whistlestop Island

Catcall Island

Warsaw Sound

ATLANTIC OCEAN

Nighthawk Island

All underlined places are fictitious.

CAST OF CHARACTERS

Alanna Hayes—A pediatric nurse who will do anything to protect baby Simon—even kidnap him and go into hiding.

Cain Caldwell—A cop who believes Alanna is responsible for his brother's death; will he turn her over to the authorities or become her personal protector?

Eric Caldwell—Cain's brother and a vigilante who put his reputation and life on the line to help abused women. Did he die for his cause?

Simon—An innocent baby who becomes a pawn in a ruthless scientific experiment called Project Simon.

Paul Polenta—A geneticist who helped Alanna escape with Simon; is he Simon's father?

Randall Ames and Stanley Peterson—Fertility specialists who created Project Simon; how far will they go to protect their secrets?

William Elk—The OB-GYN who delivered Simon. He knows the names of Simon's parents, but will he die before he reveals them?

Arnold Hughes—The former CEO of the Coastal Island Research Park. Has he resurfaced from the dead? And if so, what is his relationship to Simon?

Phyllis French—This reporter believes Simon is her baby and will do anything to get him back, even commit murder.

To Jenni and Jennifer
for not laughing when I go out on a limb
(or at least for laughing in private!).
Thanks a million.

Chapter One

Catcall Island

"Kill her," the man ordered in a gruff voice. "Then take the baby."

Alanna Hayes's heart constricted. She had to save herself, so she could save baby Simon.

Frantic, she tried to free the bindings encasing her wrists, scanning the dark interior of the lab storage room for an escape. Shadows claimed the corners, dark clouds casting bleakness through the small window, the sound of rain slashing against the metal roof ominous. Another man's husky voice filtered through the darkened doorway.

She should have known better than to snoop into unauthorized areas, but she hadn't expected the security guard to take her hostage at gunpoint. And now they'd kept her in this cold, cramped space for hours, making her wonder—

The voice broke the silence again, a harsh mumble. She didn't recognize the men's voices. Did they belong to the doctors at the research center where she worked? The security guards?

Were they really going to kill her? And what would happen to innocent little Simon? He was only four months old, he needed her....

"I don't like the idea of murder," a deep voice said.

"We have no choice," the man said matter-of-factly. "But make it look like an accident."

"What are you going to do with the baby?"

A chill rippled up Alanna's spine. The thickly accented voice belonged to her boss, Paul Polenta, one of the leading researchers in gene therapy in the country.

God, no. He couldn't be a part of this...this lab project. She'd liked him, had thought he was a brilliant, caring doctor. Just as she'd believed everyone at the Coastal Island Research Park intended to help people.

She'd been wrong.

The man's gruff voice cut through her fear like a razor blade scraping raw skin. "We're taking him to the lab as planned."

"Won't it draw suspicion if one of our nurses turns up dead?" Polenta's voice quivered. "After all, what does she really know?"

"Too much. I found her snooping in my files." The other man cleared his throat, the sound echoing beneath the eerie drone of the rain. "And I've worked too damn long on Project Simon to let some nurse destroy it. I chose her because she has no family. No one will come looking for her."

"She has a grandmother—"

"Who barely knows her name, much less if her granddaughter visits."

Alanna's chest constricted. Her grandmother had Alzheimer's. The center's research on the disease had been one thing that had led Alanna to take a job at CIRP. Even if her grandmother didn't always recognize her, Gran counted on her visits. She had no one else. What would she think when Alanna didn't show up for her weekly visit?

"But murder?" Polenta asked, sounding shaken. "We're doctors, for Christ's sake."

"Hell, man, think of your reputation. You wouldn't be able to work anywhere in the country if word leaked about this project. The Holy Rollers would picket. The press, the cops, the feds, they'd be all over us." His voice escalated several decibels. "And the government would shut us down. Then there's the damn Russians…"

Polenta grunted. "Can't we use one of those experimental drugs to alter her memory?"

"Not after the mess with that cop, Clayton Fox, and the scientist Wells and his wife. I want all loose ends tied up," the first man ordered. "Now let's get out of here. We need to be long gone when the building blows."

Outside, the rain intensified, pounding the roof with brutal force. Fear paralyzed Alanna as the voices faded into the howling wind. They were going to leave her to die. Then she'd never be able to save Simon. To hold the precious infant in her arms again.

To see him gurgle and smile. To watch him grow. To know he would have a normal life.

The outside door slammed shut. Silence followed, earth-shattering in its intensity. The low hum of a car engine sprang to life in the chilling aftermath. Thunder rumbled. Car doors closed. Gravel crunched, then tires screeched as the car peeled away.

Tears trickled down her cheeks, soaking the rag in her mouth. How long did she have before the building blew? Minutes? Seconds?

Time enough to escape? And if she did, could she find Simon and save him?

Fighting panic, she forced herself to breathe through her nose, and shuddered at the strange odor. Gas? Or was it another lethal chemical? Her heart pounding, she twisted in the chair, searching the darkness, hunting for something to help free her. Dust motes floated through the haze. Spiderwebs clung to the corners. Her eyes slowly adjusted. Lightning flashed, momentarily illuminating the sooty darkness. She searched the metal shelves and cement floor. Assorted flasks, test tubes, lab supplies.

A broken petri dish in the far corner.

She struggled to slide sideways, then slowly pushed herself up from the chair. Dizzy from the gas fumes, her legs buckled and her knees hit the concrete with a painful thud. The chair legs splintered. She winced, pitching forward, but managed to right herself, then crawled awkwardly toward the supplies.

Several long minutes later, she grasped in the dark for the broken glass and maneuvered it behind her. Thunder rent the air outside as she sawed through the thick ropes. Sweat streamed down her neck. The jagged glass jabbed her palm. Somewhere in the distance, the incessant ticking of a clock chimed. Or was it a bomb?

Her heart racing, she ignored the cramping in her muscles, the pounding in her head. Finally the rope frayed. She tugged until the ends came apart, freeing her hands.

Jerking the gag from her mouth, she heaved for air and quickly cut through the ropes around her ankles. Dizzy, she staggered to the door. Damn! It was locked. The ticking sound escalated in her head, reminding her to hurry. Then the door swung open.

A scream died in her throat.

Polenta's hulking frame stood in the shadowed awning.

"Alanna." His expression looked pained.

"Please," she whispered. "Please…don't do this, Paul. Let me take Simon and leave." She grabbed his arms, shaking him. She was crying openly now. "I love that baby, I'm the only person he knows. You can't let him be treated like a science experiment."

His jaw tightened, but he dragged her outside. Gravel crunched beneath her feet. Lightning zigzagged across the sky, illuminating his angry face. His fingers dug into her arms. Where was he taking her? Was he going to kill her himself?

She fought against him, shoving and kicking, but he slapped one hand over her mouth. "Be quiet."

Panic once again surged through her, but he pushed her down the narrow alley, then slammed her up against a black sedan. A cat screeched in the background. A low streetlight glittered off the deep puddles of water. She struggled again, but he jerked her head back so far she thought her neck would pop. Rain poured off his face, hitting her, and running off the car. Fog coated the tinted windows.

Then she saw him.

Simon was in a car seat, sleeping peacefully, his thumb tucked in his mouth. Her heart lurched. She wanted to reach out and grab the child so badly she almost doubled over.

Why was Paul doing this? Was he trying to torture her?

Suddenly he released his grip, spun her around and shoved an envelope toward her. The dark stubble on his face looked almost as abrasive as his piercing gray eyes. "There's some money and a cell phone in here in case you need to contact me. Take the baby, go to Atlanta, to Lake Lanier, and find Eric Caldwell. He'll help you."

Alanna's pulse hammered against her ribs. "You're... you're letting me take Simon?"

"I...yes." He ran a hand through sweat and rain-soaked black hair, his expression clouded with remorse. "The baby deserves a real life, not the kind they want him to have. And if Arnold Hughes resurfaces, there's no telling what he'd do."

"Oh, God, Paul, thank—"

"Don't thank me, Alanna." His bleak tone sent a shudder of terror through her. "You don't know what you're up against. When they discover you're alive, they'll hunt you down like an animal. They'll kill you just to keep you quiet.'' He gestured toward the dash. ''My pistol's in there if you need it.''

Alanna trembled at the thought. She couldn't shoot anyone. ''I can go to the police, to the papers.''

He shook his head. ''No. Don't you understand? Simon is different. We don't have time to get into the details now.'' The sound of a car backfiring in the distance jarred them both, and he opened the door. The baby stirred inside the black interior. Paul gave him a sad look, a vein throbbing in his forehead. ''If you go public, Simon won't have a chance. Every researcher across the world is going to want their hands on him for testing. And think of the press, labeling him, dogging him his whole life.''

He was right. ''Then I have to run.''

Polenta nodded, then took one long look at her, regret, confusion, resignation in his eyes. The envelope crinkled in her hands as he released it. ''You can trust Eric Caldwell, he's an old friend of mine. He works with a monastery that helps abused women obtain new identities. They can make you invisible.'' He scrubbed his hand over his neck. ''But watch out for his brother. He's a local cop, ex-military, with some kind of medical background. He might be trouble.''

She nodded, got in the car and started the engine. ''What about you, Paul?''

He placed a shaky hand on her bruised cheek. ''Don't worry about me. Just take care of Simon.'' He murmured some phrase in Spanish she didn't understand, kissed his fingers, then touched them to her hand. ''God be with you.''

Alanna gave him a last, soulful look, then put the car into gear and sped off.

Just as she exited the alley, the building exploded behind her.

Lake Lanier, Georgia
The next morning

CAIN CALDWELL PROPPED a booted foot against the doorjamb in his brother's small cabin, well aware Eric seemed to be in a hurry. Early morning sunlight settled over the dark room, highlighting his brother's gray expression. Eric was throwing together a suitcase, the bare essentials strewn across his oak bed, a cigarette dangling from his mouth. "Dammit, Eric, just tell me if you know anything about Charlene Banks."

"I told you I didn't," Eric said irritably. "And if I did, I wouldn't tell *you*. You'd probably hunt her down and arrest her instead of that sorry-ass old man of hers who beats her every other day."

Cain gritted his teeth. Damn his little brother's vigilante ways. Eric had a good heart, but his methods weren't always on the up-and-up. The very reason Cain had had to stop by. Official police business.

He jammed his hands in his pockets, forcing himself to study Eric's reaction as he made the announcement. "Her sorry-ass husband is dead."

Eric hesitated, but only for a split second, before he threw his head back and laughed. "Nice present for her. I hope he suffered like hell."

Cain silently agreed. But he was a cop, and he lived

his life by the law. He had to think in terms of black-and-white, not shades of gray, as his brother did. "Look, my captain suspects you're running some covert operations here. I can't keep covering for you."

"Covering for me?" Eric stabbed his cigarette into an empty cola can, stuffed his laptop into a black leather case, then slung the strap over his shoulder. "Is that what you call hauling my butt in for questioning three times this year?"

"They were all legitimate cases. What choice did I have?" Cain's patience snapped. "I know you're helping abused women find cover, which is not a bad thing, but what about that drug dealer who disappeared?"

"I don't know anything about him," Eric argued. "Don't you have something better to do than harass me, like look for some real crooks?"

Cain clenched his jaw. "Where's the witness in the Bronsky case, Eric?"

"What?" Sarcasm laced Eric's voice. "Did the police lose another witness?"

"We do the best we can. Do you know where he is?"

"Can't help you, bro."

"You can't go around undermining the cops and the FBI, Eric, or killing every criminal who escapes the system."

His brother glared at him, blue eyes blazing. "I didn't kill anyone."

Cain swallowed. Why did he even try? They would never see eye to eye. Yet he loved him all the same.

"I just don't want to see you get in trouble. It's

like you're on a death mission, taking everything into your own hands. One day you're going to cross the wrong people.''

''Like you don't cross the wrong kind of people all the time.'' Eric grabbed his keys off the battered dresser and strode toward the door.

''It's not the same thing. I've got people covering me. You're on your own.''

Eric hesitated momentarily, his shoulders squared. ''You could quit the force and help me. Make it your New Year's resolution.''

''New Year's has come and gone.'' Their gazes locked briefly and Cain's stomach clenched. Eric was serious.

But Cain could not straddle the line. He had sworn to uphold the law and do it honestly and he'd die trying to do just that. ''You could join the force, make enforcing the law your focus.''

''I guess we've hit that impasse again,'' Eric said quietly.

Cain clamped down on his jaw and shook his head, frustrated and worried. ''Watch your back. If you get in trouble—''

''Then you'll be there to help me.'' A cocky grin slid on his brother's face. ''Now, I'd love to stay and argue politics, but I gotta go.''

Cain caught him by the arm before he could fly past. ''Where are you going?''

Eric stared him down hard, the dark emotions in his eyes a reminder of the bond they'd shared growing up. The painful memories—the awful fights in his house, the night their mother had given up and committed suicide.

Eric had only been ten. The police had let them down then, the very reason he justified using his own methods. The reason he refused to work with the police.

But Cain had done the opposite—he'd made enforcing the law his life.

"I have business to take care of," Eric said in a quiet voice. "Legitimate business with the ranch."

Cain studied him for a long moment, then finally nodded, although he didn't believe him for a second. He released him anyway, then stood in the doorway and watched while Eric threw his bag over his shoulder, stalked down the long driveway behind his cabin to the lean-to he'd built as a carport for his Jeep. Eric had built the cover near the woods so the sun wouldn't blister his new paint job. Ironic, since the Jeep would take a mud bath going through the north Georgia mountains to get to his ranch. *If* that was where Eric was really going.

Dark clouds rolled in, obliterating the fledgling rays of sun. The wind howled off the lake, like it had the day his mother had taken her own life.

Her screams haunted him.

He shook away the thought and focused on the present. The smell of parched earth, dead leaves and something even more threatening filtered through the air. Cain's instincts screamed that something was wrong. He just couldn't put his finger on it. Like the winter storm gathering on the horizon, he had a feeling the wheels had already been set in motion.

And he had no idea how to stop them.

Cain turned to face the opposite direction, wishing one more time he could get through to his brother. Behind him, a cricket chirped, then Eric's car roared to life. Cain gripped the doorknob to shut the front door when an explosion rent the air. The wooden boards beneath Cain's feet shook with the impact.

It wasn't thunder.

Cain spun around. Horror immobilized him as Eric's car erupted into flames. He tamped down his emotions and catapulted into motion.

By the time he made it down the driveway, another explosion rocked the ground. The gas tank exploded, and fire shot into the air. Cain yelled his brother's name as he ran for the door. But heat scalded his face, the force of it knocking him backward. It was too late.

Eric was gone forever.

Chapter Two

"Hush, Simon, honey, everything's going to be all right. We're going to meet someone today who'll help us." Alanna rubbed her temple where a headache pulsed, fighting panic.

She didn't understand why Eric Caldwell hadn't met them at the Three Dollar Café for lunch as he'd promised. When she'd spoken to him last night from the hotel, he'd seemed eager to help her.

He'd advised her to disguise herself, so she'd bought a dye kit, whacked off her honey-colored hair and colored her hair black.

But she and Simon had waited for two hours at the café and he hadn't shown. She fastened Simon into the car seat, and drove away.

Staying in one place might give the men following her time to catch up. And although she had no idea who they were, she was certain they were after her. Twice, she'd spotted the same dark car behind her. But she'd managed to lose them in the rain and traffic. Was Arnold Hughes head of this secret project the scientist had been working on?

Simon twisted his tiny hands into fists, flailing them around, his face red with fury. "It's okay, honey, we'll stop in a bit and I'll see if you need changing."

She reached behind her and tried to slip a pacifier into his mouth, but he spit it out, his legs and arms circling as his sobs escalated. So did the rain.

It was coming in thick sheets now, just as it had yesterday when she'd left Savannah. Tears pressed against Alanna's eyelids, but she blinked furiously to control them and darted around a Ford pickup. More than anything she wanted Simon to have a normal life.

She'd felt an immediate bond with the four-pound infant the minute she'd seen him in the neonatal nursery, and it had grown stronger every day. Finally she'd understood how much her own mother had loved her before she died. In spite of the fact that she was a single mother, she'd tried to give Alanna everything she'd wanted. Alanna wanted to do the same for Simon. She wanted him to go to school. Have friends. Play sports.

But strange circumstances surrounded Simon's birth, which Paul wouldn't divulge. The less she knew the better, he'd said. It was safer. But why…?

How could they ever have a normal life on the run?

A knot of worry took hold in Alanna's stomach as she recalled Paul's last words, "Simon is different." How different, she wondered? What if he got sick? She'd had a fever for the past twenty-four hours, plus flulike symptoms. What if Simon grew ill? What if he had special needs that they hadn't told her about? What if he needed a doctor?

She spotted the exit sign for Lake Lanier, the area north of Atlanta where Eric lived, and drove toward the lake, squinting at the signs to make sure she didn't miss the turn. Several ski boats and houseboats came into view, and she breathed a sigh of relief, then turned onto the dirt road that supposedly led to Eric's cabin, the car bouncing over the gravel.

Five minutes later, she parked in front of the rustic-looking cabin. She had no idea why Eric Caldwell had stood them up, but she was desperate. She would beg him to help her if she had to.

THE FAINT KNOCK at the front door barely registered in Cain's mind. The rain must have stopped. Only it was still thundering in his head.

Had his partner, Neil, returned for something?

He ignored the knock, too grief stricken to move. He didn't want company now, not even his partner. The whispered condolences and sympathetic looks were more than he could bear.

Had the CSU unit forgotten to check something? Frustration clawed at him. He'd wanted to help, but the captain ordered him to stay out of the investigation, so he'd simply stared at the sooty ashes and burning embers while they'd recovered his brother's burned body.

The knock sounded again, louder this time, and he cursed. Dammit, if it was those rookies, Wade and Pirkle, telling him he had to leave his brother's cabin, he'd give them a piece of his mind.

Riddled with grief and fury, he opened the door. Instead of the rookies, a small dark-haired woman with big doe eyes stood on the steps staring up at him. An infant swathed in a blue bunny blanket squirmed in her arms.

"Mr...Caldwell?"

Her soft, feminine voice broke through his blurred haze, cutting into the pain with images of another life that might have been if he hadn't chosen police work, of sultry hot looks and sinful nights with a woman in his arms. Of a family of his own.

But Eric had been his family. And now he was gone.

"Does Eric Caldwell live here?"

He couldn't be thinking lustful thoughts, not with his brother dead. Besides, this woman looked like a drowned rat. "Yeah. I mean no." The hazy orange of dusk almost completely shadowed her face, but he catalogued her features, his detective training kicking in. Short jet-black hair plastered to her head, dark blue-green eyes, slender, attractive, almost angelic.

Scared.

She was trembling beneath that baggy, wrinkled sweater and skirt, her fine-boned hand shaking as she patted the baby's back. The bruises caught his eye. Purple and yellow ones marring her delicate wrists. Perspiration dotted her forehead and upper lip, too.

Oh, yeah, she was in trouble.

His gaze flew to her face, searching for answers. Thick black lashes curled downward over cheeks that were so pale they looked like milk. Her black hair looked unnatural, as if she'd dyed it, and the ends were tangled as if it had been aeons since she'd seen a brush. Judging from the dark circles beneath her eyes, she hadn't slept in a day or two.

She cleared her throat and he realized he hadn't answered her. "Are you Eric Caldwell?"

He stepped backward, a sudden jolt to his system he hadn't been prepared for. His throat closed momentarily, but fear radiated from her eyes and he figured she smelled the beer on his breath. She was afraid of him, he realized, a sick feeling splintering through him at the thought.

"Eric's not here." For some reason, he could not make himself say the words aloud, that Eric was dead. "I'm his brother, Cain."

"Oh." She took a wobbly step backward, the one word filled with so much disappointment that he narrowed his eyes. The baby whimpered and she crooned, murmuring nonsensical assurances in that throaty voice that tore at his gut.

"What did you want with Eric?"

Her gaze raked over him, wary and uncertain. "I...we had an appointment. He didn't make it."

The jolt slammed into him again, both sensual awareness and something else—suspicion? Eric was supposed to meet this woman today? The day he had died? Was that where he had been rushing to in such a hurry?

One look at the baby and another thought crossed his mind. Eric had so many secrets.

Or was she another one of his charity cases, running to Eric for help?

His jaw tightened with dread.

Could she possibly have something to do with his brother's murder?

ALANNA COULD NOT STOP the trembling inside her, but she made a valiant attempt to mask it in front of this man. The interior of the cabin was dark, a single light from a small lamp looming somewhere in a back room. Something was wrong. She could feel it in every fiber of her being. Despair hung in the room, heavy and intense, a mirror of her own mood.

Paul Polenta's warnings rang in her head. *Watch out for the brother. He's a cop, ex-military, medical background. He could be trouble.*

Emotions seemed to war in his eyes as he glared down at her. His black gaze was so penetrating and soulful she stepped backward, intimidated by the anger simmering beneath the surface. His potent sexuality drummed up every feminine instinct within her. And every protective one as well. She had to guard herself against him.

He was starkly handsome and one of the biggest men she'd ever met, well over six feet, with broad shoulders that pulled against the fabric of his faded black T-shirt, and hands that could probably crush a rock. Black hair framed a chiseled face that was all planes and angles and solid strength, and the thick black stubble of a five-o'clock shadow indicated he hadn't shaved today. Bronzed skin covered well-defined muscles, the heat radiating from him so powerful her belly clenched.

He'd been drinking. She smelled the beer on his

breath and, for a faint moment, wondered if alcohol affected his temperament. It didn't matter.

He was Eric Caldwell's brother. Paul had warned her not to trust him.

She should get out of there fast.

But where would she go?

She had to find Eric Caldwell.

"Come in and we'll talk." He gestured toward the shadowed foyer.

Alanna hesitated, but she slowly moved inside, hugging Simon to her. "I'd like to wait on your brother if you don't mind," she said. "It's important that I see him. Do you know when he'll be back?"

Pain flashed in his eyes. "He's not coming back."

"What do you mean?"

Instead of answering her, his voice hardened, almost defensively. He shut the door and moved in front of it. "Tell me how you know Eric, and why you were meeting him."

Renewed panic wove its way inside her. "I...I can't. It's confidential."

"You want to know about Eric, you have to talk to me, lady."

His harsh tone startled Simon. Tension escalated between them as she tried to soothe him. Oddly, Cain Caldwell shifted and jammed his hands in his pockets, his face pinched as if Simon's cries disturbed him almost as much as they did her.

Thankfully he did lower his voice. "You can start by telling me your name."

She glanced around, spotted a newspaper lying on

the hall table, and saw a headline about a Jane Doe. "Jane…Jane Carter."

A thick, black eyebrow rose in question. "How well did you know Eric, *Jane?*"

He murmured the name as if he suspected it was fake, and she shifted Simon on her shoulder, rubbing circles around his back. "Well enough," she hedged.

His other eyebrow rose. "You were involved personally?" He nodded at Simon. "And the little boy?"

Alanna opened her mouth to tell him no, then clamped down on her tongue, reminding herself not to offer too much information. If this man thought the baby was his brother's or that they'd been friends, maybe he'd help her. At least maybe he'd tell her where she could find Eric.

"I really need to talk to Eric," she said instead of answering him. "Can you just tell me where he is? Please?"

Once again that deep pain flashed into his eyes. "What's left of him is lying in a brown casket at the Bay Street Funeral Home."

Shock rippled through every nerve in Alanna's body. She shook her head, refusing to believe what he'd implied with his blunt statement.

If Eric was dead, she and Simon were all alone. They had no one to help them.

His patience snapped, and he suddenly grabbed her arms. "Yes, Ms. Carter," he said in a harsh voice. "My brother was murdered a few hours ago. His car exploded right down there, near the woods behind his house. The day he was supposed to meet you. If you know something about his murder, you'd better tell me, now.''

She glanced out the screen door and saw the marks, the charred black lines on the gravel, the yellow police tape cordoning off the area. Cain Caldwell's accusations sank in, fear spiraling through her.

Had Eric Caldwell died because he'd agreed to help her?

THE WOMAN'S FRAIL BODY shuddered within Cain's hands, and shame washed over him. The image of his brother's burned body being pulled from the wreckage of his Jeep haunted him, yet he had no right to take his grief out on this vulnerable, needy woman.

That was something his father would have done.

He had sworn he'd be a better man than his father.

He exhaled a shaky breath and released her. ''I'm sorry, Ms. Carter.'' He scrubbed a hand over his face, his throat thick. ''It's been a hell of a day.'' Of course, judging from her battered body, she'd had better days, too. Perspiration dotted her forehead, yet her hands had felt clammy. She had a fever, he realized, and wondered how long she'd been sick.

''I'm sorry about your brother.'' Panic gave the woman's voice an edge. She clutched the baby tighter and backed away. ''I...I didn't mean to bother you.''

''Wait a minute—''

''No, I have to go.'' She turned and ran, the baby's cries escalating over the howling wind as she shielded it from the rain.

''Wait, come back here!'' He ran down the porch

steps, but she slammed the car door, started the engine and tore down the driveway.

Cain's heart pounded. If she was in trouble and had come to Eric for help, he owed it to his brother to help her. And if she knew something, anything, that might tell him who had killed Eric, he had to get her to talk. Swiping a hand across his face, he grabbed his leather bomber jacket off the coatrack, yanked his keys from his pocket and ran out the back door to his car. He would follow her and see where she was headed.

Maybe she'd lead him to his brother's murderer.

Chapter Three

Someone was following her.

Like a ghost breathing down her neck, Alanna sensed them on her tail. Hovering in the distance. Watching her. Ready to pounce on her. Was it Cain Caldwell?

Or someone who wanted Simon?

Her hands tightened around the steering wheel, her heart pounding.

Rain attacked the car, the blinding whirl of water so heavy she could barely see the winding road two feet in front of her. She needed a place to stay for the night, a place to feed Simon. She had to catch her breath and think of a new plan.

Simon squirmed, his pudgy fists waging a war with the blanket she'd draped over him. The radio announcer broke into the music again with another update on the storm.

''The heavy rains are coming in off the coast of Florida, folks, a remnant of Hurricane Haley. A travel advisory is in effect for all of northern and middle Georgia.''

Great. It wouldn't let up tonight, and she couldn't cover any kind of distance in this weather. Simon cried and she tried to soothe him with her voice. She dared not drag her eyes from the road. A slow line of cars swerved and crawled in front of her, a thin thread of light from the cars behind her filtering through the fog. Thinking Simon might be cold, she turned up the heat, ignoring the fact that she was sweating. She couldn't shake this fever.

The announcer continued, "If you do not have to go out, folks, we suggest you stay inside. Power shortages have been reported in the eastern parts of the state, I-75 has been closed, and we already have several fatalities reported due to the wet conditions."

The car suddenly skidded. Alanna steered into the skid, her heart racing as she grappled for control. Simon's cries grew louder. Ahead, blue lights flashed and an ambulance wailed. An SUV spun a circle, slammed into the side of the guard rail and bounced off, sparks flying. A Suburban flew into him, the cars behind the Suburban piling up like dominoes. Metal crunched in front of her as the cars crashed into one another. Alanna slowed and swerved, barely escaping the collision.

Thank God.

But she and Simon might be here for hours.

The police would come. They might find out about him.

She had to get away.

A faded wooden post swayed amidst the blur of rain, the sign pointing to a side road that led to an old fishing lodge. It was probably empty. She could take refuge for the night, feed Simon and get on the road in the morning when the roads cleared.

Pain stabbed at her head, splintering through her body, but she ignored it. A few minutes later, she'd maneuvered the car down the dirt road to the end of a hollow and found a group of dilapidated wooden cabins interspersed amongst the newer lake property. Bundling Simon inside the blanket, she struggled up the rocky path, hunching her shoulders in the wind, trying to protect Simon from the rain. A single light burned from the rusted front of the main building. An elderly man huddled in a ratty fleece jacket greeted her at the door.

"My baby and I are stranded," Alanna yelled over the whistle of the wind. "Could we have one of your cabins for the night?"

The old man narrowed bushy gray eyebrows at her and nodded. "I'll get you a key. I've been expecting a few people tonight."

Alanna paid him in cash, accepted the key and hurried to the nearest cabin with Simon huddled in her arms. Headlights broke the foggy landscape, at least two other cars having followed her. Ducking her head so they couldn't see her, she pushed open the door to the cabin and hurried inside. Simon clutched a strand of her hair with his fist, his cries quieting slightly. The room was dark, cold and smelled of dust, but was better than sleeping in the car. Or being discovered.

She quickly locked the thin wooden door, slid the curtain aside, and looked outside at the cars beating a path up to the cabins. Simon cried again and she removed a bottle from his bag and offered it to him, grateful when he latched on and ate greedily.

"It's okay, sweetie," she crooned.

Simon stared up at her. So trusting.

He couldn't know she was lying. That she hadn't a clue as to whether or not they would survive.

Shivering, she glanced out the window at the other stranded tourists who'd veered off the road to seek shelter. The bare tree branches bowed with the weight of the wind, and several of them snapped and fell to the ground. But her eyes tracked the people as they climbed from their cars, searching their faces.

Were they all travelers stranded and lost in the storm?

Or could one of them be after Simon?

PHYLLIS FRENCH STOOD beneath the shaded cover of the neighboring porch and watched Alanna.

She had been following her since she'd left Savannah.

Smiling to herself, she patted the soft gray curls of her wig, pulled the hood of the ancient parka over her head and grabbed a bundle of wool blankets. Hunching her shoulders, she limped as she approached the cabin where the young nurse had just taken residence.

She had to see the baby for herself.

To make sure Alanna still had him. That he was safe and sound.

Phyllis placed one hand on her flat stomach where an ache burned through her belly. Emptiness clawed at her, gut-wrenching in its intensity. But she couldn't give in to the agony. She could alleviate the ache, though. When she got Simon.

And she would. She just had to be patient.

Stifling the emotions clogging her throat, she knocked on the door, knowing Alanna would be scared to open it.

"Who is it?" Alanna's thin voice barely cut through in the wind.

Phyllis masked her own voice, smiling at how well she mimicked an old lady. "It's Mr. Dimsdale's wife with extra blankets. Thought you might want them in case we lose power during the night."

The metal latch squeaked as Alanna slowly slid it open from the inside. Alanna Hayes had no idea what she'd gotten herself into. Or how to deal with the situation.

Phyllis almost felt sorry for her.

Except she had been a victim herself. Bitterness welled inside, like a virus twisting her gut into pieces. She missed her baby. Wanted him. Had to hold him.

"Miss, it's cold out here," she said, purposely letting her voice quiver.

"I'm sorry." The door finally opened a crack and the nurse peered through the narrow opening, her big blue-green eyes frightened. But her expression softened at the sight of Phyllis's stooped posture. Alanna exhaled, a tiny puff of relief Phyllis was certain the young woman hadn't realized she'd emitted.

"Thanks. My husband said you have a baby. Is the little one all right?"

Wariness darkened Alanna's features. "Why, yes... thank you for asking."

"You need anything? Formula, diapers?" Phyllis smiled, revealing fake crooked teeth. "Anything for the baby?"

"No, we're fine." Alanna opened the door just enough to take the blankets. "And thanks for these."

Wanting desperately to get a look at the baby, Phyllis tried to peer inside, but the damn woman had the door blocked. Then she heard the baby's cry. A soft little gurgling sound that squeezed at her heart.

"I'd better go feed him," Alanna said.

Phyllis nodded and fisted her hands as the door closed in her face. Despite the disappointment, excitement stirred in her chest, along with a deep longing. Ducking into the shadows of the trees, she hurried to the cabin she'd rented next door.

She would know when it was time to play her hand. When it was time to reveal herself and take Simon. And she would fight for him when that time came.

Until then, she'd be a shadow trailing Alanna Hayes's every move.

One day she would have it all. She would claim Simon as hers, the way it should have been. She would have him and everything that went along with being his mother.

Because she knew all their dirty little secrets.

The researchers'. Dr. Polenta's. Arnold Hughes's.

Even Alanna Hayes's.

CAIN SAT IN THE CAR in the blinding rain and studied the small cabin where Jane Carter, or whoever the hell she was, had hidden out for the night.

There was no question in his mind that she was hiding.

From whom, he didn't know. But she'd even acted suspicious when the old caretaker had taken her blankets.

Most likely an abusive boyfriend or husband. Eric tended to have a soft spot for women like her. They'd both known the reason why. He'd even understood Eric's actions, had wanted to cross the line a time or two himself, but he'd taken an oath to uphold the law and he intended to keep it.

Still, this woman's sudden appearance seemed too coincidental.

Did it have anything to do with Eric's death?

He parked out back near her car and settled in his seat. Surely she wouldn't be foolish enough to leave during the night, not with the bad weather and a baby in tow, and that fever. He'd sack out in the car and get some sleep and question her in the morning. If she did know something that would help him find Eric's killer, he didn't intend to lose her.

But when he closed his eyes, he couldn't shake the image of Eric's burning car from his mind.

THE CLOCK GLARED at Cain in the dimness of the predawn sky, its bold numbers mocking him with the time. Five-thirty in the morning—almost twenty hours since the explosion. Twenty hours since he'd told his brother goodbye.

He hadn't realized it would be the last time.

He folded his arms behind his head and stared at the woods, an image of the explosion, the burning car, his brother's charred remains tormenting him. They'd haunt him for the rest of his life.

Dammit, he'd told Eric that eventually something would happen to him, but even as he'd issued the warning, he'd never imagined the worst coming true, especially so soon. Eric had always managed to beat the odds. He'd acted invincible. Maybe somewhere deep down, Cain had believed it, too.

Anguish overpowered him. He'd felt helpless yesterday when his captain had ordered him to sit out the case.

Today he would start investigating.

After he made the arrangements for the memorial service.

Eric had been only twenty-nine; how could he choose a plot of land to bury his ashes in? His cell phone rang. Not wanting to listen to another awkward condolence, he let the voice mail pick up, then retrieved it in case it was important.

"Caldwell, this is Flack. Just let me know when the service is and I'll be there." Cain's captain cleared his throat, an uncharacteristic bit of emotion resonating in his voice. "And don't plan on coming in for a while. We all know you need time to deal with this. Pirkle and Wade caught the case, so try and get some rest. We'll find out who killed your brother."

A bitter snort escaped him. Rest? Like hell. He wouldn't rest until he found out who had turned his brother into a…no, he couldn't think it. And he couldn't sit around and let two half-cocked rookies handle the investigation.

Eric had devoted his life to helping victims, the vulnerable and the needy. In honor of his mother, Eric had said. If the cops had done their jobs, she wouldn't have killed herself.

What if the locals or the feds discovered his brother had taken the law into his own hands a time or two? What if Eric had something to do with Charlene Banks's husband's death?

Could Cain bring himself to cover it up to protect Eric's memory?

Jane Carter suddenly opened the door to the cabin she'd rented. She cuddled the baby to her chest and stumbled over the gravel, her face ashen, the dark circles beneath her eyes even more prominent this morning.

She was going to run. He recognized the fear in her agitated pace.

He opened the car door and stalked toward her, his gut clenching when she gripped the baby tighter and threw a terrified look his way.

FEAR SHOT THROUGH Alana at the sight of the imposing man standing before her. "You...you followed me?"

He held his hands out, palms up, to assure her he wouldn't hurt her. "I wanted to talk, that's all."

"I...I have to go."

She tried to sidestep him, but he caught her arm. "Listen, Ms. Carter, it's obvious you're in trouble. I can help you."

Huge blue-green eyes stared at him, the tension palpable as she clutched the baby protectively against her. "I don't need your help, Mr. Caldwell. I needed to see your brother."

"About what?"

She hesitated, the faint line around her mouth twitched. "That was between the two of us."

"Why won't you talk to me? Because I'm a cop?"

Her sharp intake of breath echoed in the quiet morning air. "I just want to leave." She glanced pointedly at his arm. "Now, please let me go."

He stared at her for a long minute, trying to gauge the emotions in her eyes. He wondered at the secrets. But he didn't bully women. And judging from the bruises around her arms, that was the kind of man she'd known. So he released her and took a step back, giving her space.

"I have to find the person who killed my brother." The stark need in his own voice must have gotten to her. She faltered, her pleading look full of regret and sorrow.

But fear overrode those feelings, and she reached for the car door. "I really am sorry about your brother. I wish I could help you but I can't."

Fear laced her voice, coupled with sincere remorse, which surprised him. How well had she known Eric? She strapped the baby into the car seat and started the car. When she drove away, he saw tears streaming down her cheeks.

Dammit, he wanted to help her, but she obviously didn't want his help. And he had Eric's funeral. He had to be with his brother.

Mud and rocks spewed from the back of her car as she barreled down the driveway. A green Honda pulled out behind her, a woman at the wheel. Was she following Jane or just another tourist? He memorized both license plate numbers anyway. He'd check them out later.

But now he had to go and say goodbye to his brother.

PAUL POLENTA PULLED at the leather straps holding him prisoner on the steel table, his body limp with drugs. The overhead fluorescent light glared directly at him, nearly blinding him, triggering pinpoints of pain behind his eyes. The scent of alcohol, formaldehyde and other chemicals wafted around him and he felt an icy numbness.

The irony of his situation didn't escape him. He was a genius of modern science, now trapped, a virtual prisoner of the same technology.

What had they given him? How long had he been lying here? Hours, days? Time shifted in and out of focus, as did the voices, the faces, the bare white walls. He tried to move his head to the side to determine his location, but he couldn't move. Was he in one of the research labs on Nighthawk Island? The surgical wing?

An echo of footsteps clicking on the hard floor droned into his consciousness, low, muffled voices growing nearer. He remembered talking to them. Telling them something…

They must have given him a truth serum. What had he told them? Had he mentioned Eric's name? Had he told them his address?

God, he couldn't remember.

Had they found Alanna? Simon?

In spite of the cold, beads of sweat rolled down his face. Regret swept over him almost as strong as the physical pain in his stomach. Why had he crossed the line and let them talk him into agreeing to play God? How had he ever justified tampering with people's lives?

Suddenly a blur of white moved in front of him.

Paul tried to speak, but his tongue was swollen and stuck to the roof of his mouth. Through the haze, he finally discerned the distinct lines of a man's face: the thick bulbous nose, the mole on his chin, a scar above his right eye. Peterson? Ames? Hughes? The doctor raised a hypodermic, tapped it, then lowered the needle, a frown of concentration pulling at the deep grooves of his face. Paul fought, but the weight of the drugs had paralyzed him. The needle pricked his arm, and slowly warmth seeped through his veins, numbing and languid. The light was so bright, so harsh, it swirled in a kaleidoscope of colors.

Then darkness overcame him, swallowing him into its vortex. Was he finally going to die?

Maybe it was better he did. Better to die than face the shame of his family learning what he'd done. That he'd sent them money at the sacrifice of his honor.

Alanna Hayes's beautiful face appeared in his mind's eye. He saw her holding baby Simon in his arms, cuddling the infant, rocking him good-night, whispering goodbye. He just prayed they didn't find her.

ALANNA'S THROAT CONVULSED, and clogged with tears as she sped away from the cabin. Simon flailed his hands, and she crooned to him while the winding dirt road blurred in front of her.

Where could she go now?

Although her fever-ridden body had finally given in to exhaustion around four in the morning and she'd slept for an hour, despair and fear had kept her awake most of the night.

Eric Caldwell was dead.

The grief and pain in his brother's eyes had nearly ripped the last vestiges of her control right from her. She'd wanted to tell him everything. To plead for his help. But something had stopped her.

She spared a glance at Simon who popped his chubby thumb into his mouth and began to suckle it. He trusted her to take care of him.

But could she live up to his trust?

The only person in the world she'd thought could help them was a stranger who had been killed the same day he was supposed to meet her.

Guilt pressed heavily against her.

What was she doing to do now? How could she possibly keep Simon safe and give him a new life without Eric Caldwell's help? And how could she live with his death on her conscience?

Chapter Four

The brisk January wind tossed brown leaves across the graveyard, the whistle of winter a bitter reminder of the emptiness that had settled inside Cain's chest. Head bent, hands shoved deep into the pockets of his faded leather jacket, he stared at the ground where his brother's remains lay, the steel gray of the casket the same drab color as the clouds hovering above.

The gatherers were sparse. It was a sad testament to Eric that he had so few friends. Yet he had helped so many nameless, faceless strangers who had drifted through his life for a day or week until he could help them move on. They might mourn him if they were still around. Or if they dared come out of hiding. But they didn't.

A few of Cain's friends from the police force had turned out for the memorial service, more out of respect for him than his brother, since half the force had had run-ins with Eric over the past two years.

They hadn't seen Eric's good side like he had. They hadn't known that the man who pretended not to care about anyone or anything, the hardened renegade who crossed the line and had little regard for the law, was really a tender heart inside, risking his life and reputation to give hope to abused women.

Cain's throat ached from grief, and his cheeks stung from the wind sifting through the limbs of the nearby trees.

The minister offered a few words of prayer, the same mindless mutterings that should offer hope to those left behind, but Cain felt too numb and angry to be comforted.

"You doing okay?" Captain Bobby Flack laid a broad hand on Cain's shoulder.

Cain shrugged. What could he say? *Hell no, I watched my brother get blown up, and couldn't do anything to stop it.* Cain was the oldest; he should have protected him...

"You need some time off, Caldwell. Take it."

Cain shot him a dark look. He didn't want time off. He wanted to be on the case and Flack damn well knew it.

The scrape of dirt being hoisted into shovels and thrown onto his brother's casket jerked his attention back to the grave. His co-workers shuffled by, one by one, heads bowed, voices low as they offered their condolences. Cain nodded and grunted, knowing the men didn't expect any more. Not that the officers didn't face their own mortality every day; probably why it made them all so damn uncomfortable to attend a funeral.

"We'll get the person who did this," Wade said as he moved past.

"Hang in there, man," Pirkle added.

Cain's throat closed as the mound of dirt grew higher. From his pocket he pulled the gold cross that had belonged to Eric, and ran his thumb over the worn, cool gold, remembering the day his mother had given it to his brother. Eric's thirteenth birthday.

Eric had already started to develop an attitude. He'd gotten into several scrapes and brawls at school, had beaten up some bully who'd been picking on a younger girl. They'd come home from school that day and found their mother bruised and battered again, lying on the sofa with an ice pack on her face. Their father had left, Eric's birthday not even a speck of dust in his memory.

Furious over his mother's black eye, Eric had wanted to tear out of the low-rent flat where they'd been living and charge after his dad, but his mother had told him he couldn't leave, not on his birthday. Then she'd shown him the homemade cake she'd baked and given him the cross. Cain could still see the tears in her eyes as she'd hung the cross around his neck.

"This is to remind you of the good in the world, so you don't grow up to be like your father," she said.

And Eric hadn't. He might not have followed the letter of the law, but he hadn't deserved to die the way he had.

Someone had to pay for his death. And if Cain found whoever had killed him, he would take care of them himself. To hell with his badge. He wanted justice. No—he wanted more than that.

He wanted revenge.

SIMON'S SMALL SOUNDS of hunger grew more incessant over the miles.

"I'll feed you when we reach the monastery," Alanna promised. "We'll be there soon, honey." Alanna struggled to remain calm as she veered from the winding road onto the highway that led to Buford.

Simon continued to fret over the next few miles, the countryside changing to suburbia. She glanced at her rearview mirror, trying to decide if the dark car was following her or if she'd finally succumbed to paranoia.

When she'd left Cain Caldwell, she'd debated whether to return to the lake cabin, but she was afraid he'd show up, probing for more information on Simon. This morning she'd remembered Paul telling her that Eric Caldwell had helped women go underground through a local monastery in Buford, and she'd searched the phone book for a number. Thankfully, there was only one listed in the small town, although there were several others in and around the city of Atlanta.

Headlights flashed ahead, nearly blinding her, but she managed to stay on the road, Simon's cries escalating. "Hang on, sweetie, we're almost there." She checked the directions, then the numbers along the street, grateful to see the side road that led to the monastery. She turned down the road, then steered the car into the long driveway, her stomach knotting as Simon's wails increased. A huge stone structure surrounded by black iron gates sat back from the road, woods surrounding it. Although the building seemed imposing, she had no choice. She needed help and she had nowhere else to turn.

Simon was screaming now, thrashing his fists and hands wildly. She stopped in front of the building, but darkness shrouded the stone structure, and the mixture of overgrown weeds and dead leaves and broken rock near the awning was not a good sign. Neither was the broken glass in the window to the side or the spiderwebs climbing like vines up the walls of the building.

The building had obviously been abandoned.

She was just about to drop her head and give in to tears when a dark sedan crept up the driveway toward her. Dear God. The car *had* been following her.

Adrenaline and self-preservation kicked in. She shoved the car into Drive, hit the gas and took off, passing the car and flying toward the highway. She tightened her hands around the steering wheel as the screeching tires roared behind her. Swerving onto the main road, she drove like a demon.

But a few minutes later, she bumped across the railroad tracks just before the railroad crossing warning dinged. Then the crossing rails lowered and trapped the sedan, and she breathed a sigh of relief.

The shrill sound of her cell phone cut into her reprieve. Alanna's heart raced as she glanced at it. Was Paul calling her?

Hands shaking, she answered it. "Hello?"

"Ms. Hayes, this is a friend of Eric Caldwell's."

Her breath hitched. "You worked with Eric?"

"Yes. He told me about your call. I know he was supposed to meet you the day he died."

Relief spilled through her. "You work for the same organization as Eric?"

"Yes. He gave me your cell number in case he couldn't reach you."

"I went to the monastery but it was closed."

"I know. Meet me at the cemetery where Eric is buried." He recited short directions in a clipped voice. "And make sure you're not followed."

"I will. Thank you." She checked her rearview mirror and drove toward the graveyard. Thank heavens Eric had told someone else about her. Maybe they could help her and Simon escape.

CAIN HAD TRIED TO LEAVE the cemetery several times, but each time his legs had refused to work. Now he sat on the ground beside the fresh mound of dirt with his head down, so swamped with childhood memories of Eric that he could barely breathe.

He caught the flicker of a gray parka in his peripheral vision and glanced sideways.

Jane Carter, the woman with the baby, had come to Eric's grave. Her frail figure stood like a ghost in the shadows of the trees only a few feet away. The baby lay bundled in her arms, her shivering form a staunch reminder of the terror he'd seen in her eyes that morning and the day before.

He had to know why she'd come.

And why she'd been drawn to his brother's grave when she'd been in such a hurry to escape from him this morning.

ALANNA ROCKED the baby in her arms, shielding him from the howling wind with her coat as she searched the graveyard for the man who'd phoned her.

She spied a man sitting hunched over on the ground beside Eric's grave. Was it Cain or the man who had called to help her?

Gravel crunched behind her, the footfalls of someone approaching sending a chill up her spine. She turned around, half expecting the men in the black car to have dogged her, but the shadow of a woman deep in the heart of the knotty pines flickered. Alanna couldn't distinguish the woman's face or anything else about her, except that she wore black. Maybe she worked for the organization, too. Or was she just a mourner?

Then the man turned and looked straight at her and she realized it was Cain. The anguish in his eyes nearly made her legs buckle.

She couldn't let him see her. Alanna pivoted and started back to her car, but before she reached it, Cain caught up with her and grabbed her arm.

"I thought you were headed out of town." Cain Caldwell's hulking body towered over her, and Polenta's warning rang in her head. *Be careful of Eric's brother. He had some military background, medical training. Don't let him know about Simon.*

"I am. But I thought I'd stop and pay my respects to your brother." Not much of a lie, but she was so rattled she couldn't think.

"So you knew Eric well?"

She shrugged, not knowing how to answer. Eric had had a nice voice. She just prayed he truly hadn't died because of her.

A drop of sleet hit Cain Caldwell's cheek, another pelted the ground below. Dead leaves fluttered into his black hair, across his leather jacket and onto the ground, but he seemed oblivious to the cold or the weather. Except for the black irises of his eyes. They burned with an intensity that seared her.

"Your brother was a good man," she said, knowing in her heart it was true. He had planned to help her. No questions asked.

"Yes, he was." His jaw twitched slightly, the only indication her comment had affected him. "Not everyone realized that, though. Sometimes he liked to straddle the line of the law."

"He…I'm so sorry he's gone."

Again that twitch in his jaw. "Tell me why you're here." His gaze flickered over her. Then Simon.

As if Simon realized he was being scrutinized, he squirmed in her arms, one fist sneaking out of the blanket. She tucked it back and soothed him, not wanting the cold air to touch his skin.

"I…I need to go." She gestured toward Simon. "I don't want him to get sick."

She moved quickly to escape him, but Cain pulled her toward him, holding her so close his breath bathed her face. He'd obviously neglected to shave, and the dark stubble of his beard looked abrasive. She heard his teeth grind as he clenched them.

"It's no coincidence that someone murdered my brother the same day you showed up needing help," he said in a low growl. "Tell me what you're afraid of and who you're running from."

She had no idea what to do or what to tell him. But his fingers dug into her arms tighter, almost to the point of pain. If he thought she had caused his brother's death, would he take his anger out on her? Would he turn Simon over to the scientists searching for him or expose his birth circumstances publicly?

A shudder coursed through her. She could not let him do that to Simon.

His grip tightened as he stared deeper into her eyes. The way the guards on Nighthawk Island had handled her, their brutal force and threats suddenly rushed back, haunting her. She jutted her chin in the air, hoping the shiver in her body didn't betray her show of bravado. "I'm running from men like you." She purposely lowered her eyes to his hand where his fingers held onto her.

His gaze dropped to his hand, too, and he went still. He released her so suddenly that she stumbled backward, then caught herself and leaned against the tree to calm her nerves.

"I'm sorry." His apology gushed out, so quick and gruff that she blinked to make certain she'd heard it. Then she saw him glance at the bruises on her wrist, and his anger transformed into regret. He held his hands up and frowned at them, then stepped away from her, as if to give her the freedom to leave if she wanted. "I won't hurt you."

She nodded stiffly, as uncomfortable with this tender side as she had been with his gruff exterior.

"I simply want some answers." He jerked his head toward the mound of his brother's grave. "He was my baby brother. My...my only family." He cleared his throat, pain lacing his thick voice. "I...I have to know who killed him."

Alanna closed her eyes, the raw grief in his words pulling at her heartstrings. How could she help him without endangering herself or Simon? Polenta's warnings reverberated over and over in her head. She couldn't trust him…

"A…an ex-boyfriend is after me. He…" Lies tumbled through her mind. What would he believe? What would make him want to help her, not harm her or Simon?

"He's the one who hit you?"

She nodded, shame washing over her for deceiving him. But Simon's safety was the only thing that mattered. "I'm afraid he'll hurt the baby."

"The baby's his?"

Before she could answer, a gunshot pierced the air. Cain pushed her and Simon behind a tree, and they both hit the ground, shielding Simon with their bodies.

Chapter Five

Cain's jaw snapped tight. Who were these thugs? Why would they try to gun down an innocent woman and baby?

He pulled out his own weapon and aimed, then fired, sending the bullet into a tree only a few feet from the men's heads. Jane screamed and the baby cried out.

The men froze. He fired again, this time hitting a lower tree branch that splintered and fell to the ground. He aimed the next one into the ground at the bald man's feet. He reached for his cell phone to call for backup, but the men turned and ran toward their car, both heaving for air and looking over their shoulders in fear. His gaze swung back to Jane. She had scrambled behind a low bush, trying to quiet Simon but to no avail. Cain waited several seconds until the men's car tore from the parking lot, then slipped as quietly as he could toward her. Seconds later, she raised her head and peered through the brush, cuddling Simon close as she searched for the men. He gently placed his hands on her arms. "Jane—"

She jerked to a standing position, ready to run.

"It's okay now, they're gone." She was shaking so badly he did the only thing he could.

He pulled her and Simon into his arms and offered her comfort.

ALANNA FELL INTO Cain's arms, knowing she should resist but unable to help herself from accepting the safety of his strong embrace. She'd been running scared for days with nowhere to turn, and she had come so close to losing Simon.

The phone call had been a setup. How had the men gotten her number and known about her contact with Eric? She should get rid of the phone—

Paul. Dear God, she couldn't. It was her only way of staying in touch with him.

Simon seemed to calm, his cries quieting. Cain stroked his back in slow rhythmic motions, murmuring soft words of reassurance.

A tear threatened to escape but she blinked it back. She couldn't allow herself the weakness.

"Are you all right?" Cain asked softly.

Alanna nodded against his chest, finally pulling away enough to look into his eyes. Simon angled his head toward her, then toward Cain as if to ask why someone would try to hurt them. Alanna kissed the baby gently on the cheek. "It's okay, Simon. Everything's all right now."

"Who were those men?" Cain brushed at a leaf caught in her hair. "And don't tell me one of them was your old boyfriend."

She clutched Simon's pudgy finger and disengaged

herself from Cain's arms, already missing his warmth and strength. "I don't know."

"Why are they after you?" His voice was low, but his gaze dared her to lie.

"I…my ex-boyfriend must have hired them to find me."

"To gun you down?" Not that he hadn't seen it all before. But he didn't believe her.

"He wants me to come back." She stumbled backward. "He's obsessed…"

Cain steadied her. "Come on, you're going home with me tonight."

"No—"

"Don't argue with me, Jane. You damn near got yourself killed. No telling what could have happened to Simon." He reached out and laid a palm against Simon's cheek. "The baby needs a safe place for a while. And I want some answers."

"Thanks for rescuing us, Cain, but I can't stay with you."

He took her arm and ushered her toward her car, ignoring her protests. But as they reached it, he pulled her past the door. "We'll come back for your car later."

"No." She might need to escape later. She needed her own wheels. "I can't leave the car here."

"Then I'll send one of my buddies after it."

One of his cop friends? "Then you'd have to tell them about me and Simon."

"Yes. And if you'll give me the name of this old boyfriend and a description, I'll issue an APB for him."

She halted, gathering all her strength to remain still when he tried to urge her forward. "You can't do that, Cain. Please. Just let me go."

"I'm not letting you drive off tonight with Simon. And if you don't level with me about Eric, I'll haul you in for withholding information in a murder investigation."

"Please, Cain, no."

"This obsessive boyfriend of yours might have followed you here and killed my brother." He hesitated, obviously reading the panic in her face.

But his steely gaze didn't waver. "If you don't want me to call the police in, then when we get back to my place, you have to tell me what's going on." He gave her directions to the cabin.

She reached for the door handle. Cain grabbed it first, wrapping one arm around her. "And don't get any ideas about running, Jane. I'm going to be right behind you."

CAIN'S PULSE CLAMORED as he jumped in his Jeep. Sleet pelted the windshield, the bitter wind picking up. Trying to stay on Jane's tail, he turned on the defroster as the car flew over the ruts in the dirt road.

The same small dark green Honda turned off the dirt road onto the highway and he caught a glimpse of black inside—was the woman following her?

Peering through the fogged windshield, he stayed right behind Jane's Toyota. He tried to get a good look at the person in black inside, but the Honda suddenly pulled into a convenience store and he realized

he must have been wrong about the car following Jane.

Still he called in the plates along with Jane's. A
few minutes later, he learned the Honda belonged to
a woman named Phyllis French. She had no priors,
no record, nothing unusual about her at all.

The car Jane drove belonged to a doctor named
Paul Polenta. He had no record either, and the car
hadn't been reported stolen. So who was this Polenta
guy? Was he the old boyfriend who'd been stalking
her? Another lover?

DAMN.

Irritated, Phyllis slipped into the convenience store,
grabbed a disposable cup and filled it with coffee. The
man Alanna Hayes had gone to see was either a cop
or working with them. She'd recognized the standard
weapon and the badge clipped on his outside coat
pocket.

The cop was also following Alanna.

He'd spotted *her* as well.

So had Alanna Hayes at the graveyard, though the
woman had no idea who she was or that she wanted
Simon just as badly as the men searching for her.

Phyllis stirred cream into the coffee, then added a
packet of sugar. The cop hadn't seen her face. And
even if he had, he couldn't know anything about her
connection to the Hayes woman. No one did.

As far as the scientists back on Nighthawk Island
were concerned, Phyllis had disappeared from their
lives after her miscarriage. But she hadn't. She'd sus-

pected something strange about their work. Then she'd found out about those fertility treatments....

Why the hell would Alanna Hayes go to the police? The stupid nurse had to know the danger in doing so. She would have been better off going to the press. And if she'd told that cop her story, why hadn't he taken her in for kidnapping?

Brahms's ''Lullaby'' floated into her head. She'd hummed the song to her unborn child during her pregnancy. She'd intended to sing her baby to sleep with it every night. But now Alanna had Simon, cuddling and rocking him at night, when it should have been her.

Those bastards on Nighthawk Island had kept Simon from her long enough.

Phyllis would make them pay.

Grabbing a newspaper from the bin on the wall, she stepped to the counter to pay.

''Will that be all, ma'am?''

Phyllis nodded.

''Four fifty-five.''

She threw down a five-dollar bill, then rushed out the door. She'd already lost precious minutes hiding in the store. She couldn't afford to waste any more, or she might lose her only connection to Simon.

But before she made her move, she had to find proof that Simon belonged to her. So they'd never be able to steal him from her again.

A HALF HOUR LATER, Cain stood in his kitchen heating a can of soup while Jane fed Simon. The baby gurgled and spit rice cereal everywhere, then lapped up the peaches with gusto as Jane spooned them into his mouth. She had been suspiciously quiet, avoiding conversation with him, focusing all her attention on the baby.

Cain would let it ride for now.

But when Simon went to bed, they had to talk.

He filled the bowls with steaming chicken noodle soup and placed one on the table in front of her, the other at the opposite end for himself. He added crackers and poured them both some coffee, then set the sugar and milk on the table, and took the seat at the end of the table.

He had not been around babies much, but Simon seemed happy and well cared for in spite of their earlier ordeal. Jane, on the other hand, was a mess.

He didn't want to think about the strong urges he'd felt when she'd pressed herself into his arms. Protective instincts had mushroomed alongside sexual feelings that had no place between them.

Especially if she was involved in Eric's death.

Simon suddenly blew bubbles, spraying Jane's shirt. Jane laughed, a soft, lighthearted, totally content and motherly sound that pinched his stomach. Even pale and frightened, she'd draw any man's eye, but with a smile on her face she looked absolutely beautiful.

"I think you've had enough." Jane wiped Simon's chin with a paper napkin. "Now how about some milk to wash it all down?"

Simon cooed a reply while she laid him back in her arms and slipped the bottle into his mouth. Like an experienced mother, she angled herself to sip her coffee and eat at the same time.

"Looks like you've done that before." Cain couldn't keep a grin from sliding onto his face.

She smiled at him, actually blushing. "Seems like babies always want to eat when the adults do." She shrugged, her green sweater slipping off one shoulder. "I don't mind, though. He's good company."

"It's obvious you love him very much."

"I do."

"Did you and this ex-boyfriend break up before you met Eric?"

She stiffened, then sipped her coffee again. "Yes. He was stalking me and I asked Eric for help. That's how we met."

He nodded, admitting the plausibility of her story. But she didn't quite meet his eyes when she spoke.

"Why didn't you want me to call the police? You can issue a warrant for this guy, get a restraining order—"

"I've done all that before." She stood and rocked Simon from side to side. He was falling asleep in her arms, one hand curled against the bottle. "Is there someplace I can let him rest for the night?"

"This way."

Cain's cabin consisted of two bedrooms with a shared bath and an open room that served as the den, with an attached kitchenette. A faded green sofa and comfortable recliner occupied the den along with a TV and his ancient stereo system. He normally didn't bring women here. They found it too rustic.

"Is he crawling yet?"

"Not yet," she whispered. "Although he's trying."

"So, he'll be okay on the bed?"

"I'll put some pillows beside him so he doesn't roll off." She gently pulled the bottle from Simon's hand and kissed him on the forehead while Cain turned down the navy comforter. Then she eased Simon onto the bed, brushing a tender hand over his belly as he stretched his chubby arms and legs. Light blond eyelashes fluttered once, but he didn't wake.

"He's so tired. It's been a trying day."

"I imagine so. It's not every day a baby gets shot at."

He heard her sharp intake of breath. As soon as they made it back to the small den, he turned to her.

That haunted look returned to her eyes. "We'll be out of your way in the morning."

"You aren't going anywhere." Cain folded his arms. "Now, just before those goons showed up you were going to tell me about Simon's father."

ALANNA WAS EXHAUSTED, but she couldn't give in to it. Even though she'd told Cain she and Simon would leave tomorrow, she had no idea where they would go. With Eric dead, the monastery abandoned and the men after her close on her tail, how would she possibly escape? She was in way over her head. Completely out of her element.

And Cain Caldwell was demanding answers.

What would make him want to protect Simon instead of turning him over to the men looking for him or to the police? There was only one thing....

"Who is his father, Alanna?"

She hesitated, gathering courage, praying God could somehow forgive her for what she was going to say. "The baby, well…Eric is Simon's father."

Chapter Six

"What?"

"I know it's hard to believe."

The anguish Cain had felt earlier intensified as he stared at the woman in shock. Her eyes flickered with unease as if she feared his reaction, and shame filled him for being rough with her earlier.

He refused to be like his father.

This was one reason he'd kept himself focused on his job and had never let himself get too close to anyone before.

Was she telling the truth? Had his brother fathered the little boy sleeping in his spare room?

Eric normally didn't get involved with the women he helped. He didn't want to take advantage of them in their vulnerable state.

Had Eric known about Simon or had he died before he'd learned of his existence?

"Are you sure he's Eric's son?"

Anger tightened her mouth, and he realized the implication of his question.

"Yes, but I don't expect anything...I didn't come

here to cause trouble." She reared her head back. "And I didn't want anything from Eric except for him to help me find a safe place to take Simon."

"Did he know about the baby?"

She chewed her bottom lip. "No. I told him I had a child and that we needed help. I intended to tell him the rest when I got here."

So, Eric had died without knowing he had a son. Cain's chest constricted. "Why did you keep it from him?"

She shook her head, that wariness back in her eyes. "It's a long story. I...I was afraid." The arm of her long-sleeved sweater rode up as she lifted her arm.

"Afraid of what your boyfriend might do? Is it Polenta?"

A gasp escaped her. "How do you know about Paul?"

"Is he your old boyfriend?"

"No, he's...a friend. He loaned me his car so I could leave town. But how did you know?"

"I'm a cop, Jane. I ran the plates on the car."

She nodded, shaken. "What else did you find out?"

"Nothing. But it's time you filled me in."

"I told you, an old boyfriend is after me. I haven't been with him in ages but he wouldn't leave me alone. He couldn't stand the thought of me with someone else."

"Do you think he killed Eric?"

"No. I...he didn't know Eric's name." She twisted her hands together. "But I'm worried about Simon."

He arched a brow, zeroing in on her panicked gaze.

"You think he might hurt the baby because he's Eric's?"

She nodded, though her gaze didn't quite meet his. His protective instincts quickly roared to life. He knew exactly how it felt to take the brunt of a man's rage, to feel the print of his hand on his face.

And so did this woman.

He tried to picture her with Eric, tried to remember Eric mentioning a woman, but nothing concrete came to mind. Of course, they'd spent the past few months arguing half of the time.

So much time wasted.

If this baby was Eric's, he couldn't let her leave. Not when she was sick and looked like she might blow over any second.

Not when the baby was the only link he had left to his brother.

He just wished he knew the rest of the story.

He had to help her. But he wasn't like Eric, and she would discover that soon enough. He lived by the letter of the law.

If she was lying to him, he'd find out the truth about that as well. And *if* her alleged boyfriend had found Eric and killed him, then Cain would find him and make sure he paid.

More questions plagued him. Had she loved his brother? Had Eric been in love with her?

ALANNA FOUGHT THE URGE to run. She had just told this man that the baby in his guest room was his brother's son, *his* nephew. He was bound to want to touch him, hold him.

But would he be able to look into Simon's eyes and see the truth?

"How old is he?" Cain asked in a voice thick with emotion.

"Four months." Alanna forced a smile. "He's really a good baby."

"Spoken like a true mother."

A tremor tore through her, but he didn't notice. "He *is* good, but he must sense the tension."

She pushed the short hair from her face, the wispy dark strands another reminder of her situation. And his.

Of course his emotions were volatile right now. He'd just lost his brother and thought he'd found his brother's son; shame washed through her at her deception. The man needed comfort.

But she was the wrong person to give it to him.

"So I have a nephew." A small smile twitched at the corner of Cain's mouth, his hard features transforming into something else—something much more dangerous. Cain Caldwell was one of the most powerfully masculine men she'd ever met.

She must be more exhausted than she'd realized, she thought. For a moment, she'd forgotten the cold and fear surrounding her, that if she let her guard slip, this man could turn her over to the authorities.

She'd forgotten he'd looked so desolate earlier by his brother's grave and that she might be responsible for putting the anguish in his eyes. And now, if he found out she'd lied about Eric being Simon's father, he would hate her.

Torn over accepting his protection and feeling

guilty about her deception, Alanna knew she had to leave in the morning. If Eric had been killed because of her, then anyone who helped her would be in danger. She couldn't live with another man's death on her conscience.

CAIN WANTED TO ASK her more questions, but he saw fatigue lining her face, heard the tremor in her voice, and knew it could wait. She looked as if she might collapse any second.

In the morning, he'd find out the boyfriend's name.

He led her back to the guest room where Simon lay on the pine bed occupying the corner.

"Do you need anything for the night?" He gestured toward the duffel bag he'd brought in for her earlier, but she shook her head.

He moved to the door to offer her some privacy. "Jane…"

She turned, her eyelids already drooping. "Yes?"

"If you need me, just call."

She seemed startled for a minute, as if his offer was so foreign she didn't know how to respond, adding questions to the already growing pile he had about the men in her life. Then she nodded and he closed the door behind him.

The diaper bag she'd brought in sat on the end table oddly out of place. He hadn't seen her with a purse, so he rummaged through the bag searching for ID. A driver's license would at least reveal her real name. But he found nothing inside but baby paraphernalia. Damn. Then his hand connected to cold metal.

Recognition dawned. A gun.

Slowly he pulled out the small pistol, checking to make sure the safety was on. What in the hell was she doing with a gun? Did she have a license for it?

Deciding to hedge his bets, he took the weapon and locked it in his own desk. He tiptoed down the hall and peeked through the crack in the door. She lay on her side, her back facing him, one arm thrown over the baby. Her motherly love touched chords deep within him, resurrecting painful memories of his mother. Of her depression, her weakness, her lack of assertiveness in fighting for him and Eric.

Who was this fragile but courageous woman?

Today she had fought for herself and her child. Even in her sleep, she was protecting Simon.

His nephew?

Was she as vulnerable as she appeared or could she be in trouble with the law herself?

He eased over to the bed and stared at the little baby. His heart ached, fresh grief suffusing him. Eric would have loved a son.

Had his brother been in love with the baby's mother as well?

SOMETHING WAS WRONG. The scent of parched earth, of dry dead leaves, of danger filtered through the cold air. "I have to go." Eric slung his backpack over his shoulder and shot him that devilish grin that dared him to question his motives.

"Dammit, Eric, come back here." Cain watched his brother walk down the driveway toward his Jeep, dark clouds obliterating the sun and casting shadows

along his face. Trees flanked the lean-to where he stored the Jeep.

Cain's frustration mounted. But he let him go. It was futile to fight. He had turned to close the door when a loud thunderous sound rent the air. He spun around, horror shaking him to the core. No!

Eric's car had exploded. Flames shot up, grabbing the wooden lean-to. Cain took off at a dead run, his heart pounding in fear. His feet skidded on gravel and another explosion rocked the ground. Glass shattered and spewed across the dirt. The smell of smoke and gasoline knocked him backward.

He raced to the car. He had to get Eric out. But heat seared him. The fire blazed out of control, crackling and eating the metal. Then the rubber tires. He reached for the door but flames engulfed the entire vehicle.

A cry of rage tore from his chest and he dropped to his knees. White-hot heat scalded his face as he watched the flames shoot into the dark sky. It was too late.

Eric was gone forever.

CAIN JERKED AWAKE and sat up in his bed, his breathing labored, his pulse racing. He'd been dreaming.

No, the dream had been real.

Pain knifed through him and he doubled over, fighting the grief swelling inside him.

He had to know who had killed his brother.

Today he would call Detectives Wade and Pirkle, see if they'd made any headway on the investigation.

And if they hadn't, he'd push them to try harder. He'd go down there and take over the investigation himself. To hell with time off.

The image of Jane Carter lying in the guest room flashed unbidden in his mind. His sex stirred at the thought of her slim, delicate body stretched beneath the sheets. He could not lust after a woman in trouble, especially one who had slept with his brother and given birth to his brother's child.

Or caused him to die.

He grabbed his shirt and jeans and pulled them on, then walked to the den and paced to the kitchen to make coffee. He'd check the computers, see if he could find anything about a missing woman and child listed on the state database. And he'd find out who the gun belonged to, if Jane had a license to carry one.

The coffee began a steady drip from the machine. A beam of early morning sunlight reflected off the appliances. But even the bright sunlight couldn't obliterate the darkness in his soul. His gaze shot back to the room where Jane Carter slept. Once upon a time, he would have tried to wipe out that darkness with a woman.

But the only thing he and Jane Carter could share was their concern for Simon.

Still, she might hold the answers to Eric's killer. And he wouldn't let her out of his sight until he dragged the truth out of her.

ALLANA SHOT UP off the bed, certain she'd heard someone cry out in pain. At first she'd thought it was

Simon, but she leaned over and checked him and he was sleeping peacefully. Had the sound come from Cain's bedroom? Or maybe she'd woken herself with the silent scream she hadn't been able to get past her throat. She'd been running in the woods with Simon, the men had tried to steal him....

But it hadn't been a dream.

The early strains of sunlight flitted through the blinds, drawing soft white lines across Simon's cheek. She smiled and stroked a finger across his baby-fine hair.

The first time she'd laid eyes on him in the hospital at CIRP he'd stolen her heart. She had bonded with him immediately, as strong as if she had been the one to give him life. He had been motherless and she had been aching to fill the emptiness in her own life, so it had been natural for her to take care of him, so natural that she hadn't asked questions.

She'd trusted too easily.

Only then she'd discovered the lies....

CAIN HELD a mug of black coffee in his hands as he watched the morning news. As soon as Jane woke up, he'd get some answers.

The freezing rain and sleet had iced over two bridges that were closed across the Chattahoochee. A bomb threat had caused a stir at a high school in Fulton County so the kids were being held in the gym.

"And now, this late-breaking story," a newscaster announced. "Police in Savannah, Georgia, report that renowned geneticist Paul Polenta was discovered injured in his research lab at the Coastal Island Research Park on Catcall Island. Polenta is reportedly in a coma at this time in ICU. Police are searching for a woman named Alanna Hayes for questioning. Ms. Hayes was hired as a nurse to take care of Polenta's infant son, Simon, but four days ago, the baby was taken from Polenta's home.

"Since the abduction, police have learned that Ms. Hayes was recently divorced. Co-workers at the research hospital speculate that Ms. Hayes was distraught over learning she could not have children of her own, became obsessed with Polenta's child and fled with the baby.

"If you have any news regarding this woman and child or their whereabouts, please phone your local police."

A photo of Alanna Hayes and the baby flashed on the TV. Cain stared in shock, his coffee cup clattering onto the table. The photograph showed a very blond Jane Carter.

Chapter Seven

Alanna stared at the TV in disbelief, her heart racing. Dear God, she had to get out of here. Everyone would be looking for her...

Cain's stunned and angry gaze pinned her to the spot.

She backed up slowly, ready to run, the news report echoing over and over in her head. They had made her out to be some kind of psycho who'd stolen Simon out of a sick need to possess a child. Why would the people at CIRP broadcast Simon's disappearance? Weren't they afraid she'd go to the police or to the media?

No, they knew she would never expose Simon to such a circus. And now that she'd been put on the defensive, the police would never believe her.

The scientists were smart—they intended to get rid of her and make themselves appear to be the good guys.

She stumbled over a rough spot in the flooring and her back hit the wall. Cain stalked toward her, his six-foot-plus height filled with animosity. Panicking, she turned to run but Cain swung her around, trapping her against the wall. His dark eyes bored into her, and his broad jaw was clenched so tightly a muscle ticked at the corner of his mouth.

"You've been playing me like a guitar string, *Alanna*," he said in a deceptively calm voice. "You put my brother's life in jeopardy and involved him in a felony kidnapping."

"It's not like that—"

"Really? Then you have five minutes to tell me how it is, or I'm turning you in."

"I...it's not true. I'm not the sick woman they say I am."

"Then you admit that you took Simon from that doctor?"

She clenched her teeth, struggling with how much she dared tell him. "Yes, but it's not the way they said on the news."

"Simon is not my brother's son, is he?"

A heartbeat of silence stretched between them. Long enough for her to see the anguish she'd caused him. He had wanted the baby to be his brother's so he'd have something left of Eric.

She shook her head slowly, tears pooling in her eyes. "No. I'm s-so sorry."

He closed his eyes, another pain-filled silence stretching between them as he fought for control. His breath brushed her cheek and the sound of his rapid breathing filled the air.

"I didn't want to lie to you about that," she whispered. "But I...I didn't know what else to do. I thought if you believed Simon was Eric's son you'd help me.''

He opened his eyes and searched her face, anger warring with anguish. "Help you kidnap a child from his rightful parents? I'm a cop, for God's sake. I can't be a party to a federal crime." He reached for the phone but she grabbed his arm, near hysteria.

"But wait, you can't—"

"Is that the reason you have a gun?"

"You went through my things?"

"Yes."

She tried to run, but he stopped her. "Why do you have the gun?"

"To protect myself and Simon. He doesn't have anyone but me."

"You have a license for it?"

"It's Paul's gun."

"Paul?"

"Dr. Polenta. He gave it to me when I took off with Simon."

"You're not Simon's mother. You're a nurse who was hired to take care of him?"

Her heart ached to have to admit that he was right. "Yes."

His sound of disgust was so sharp he might as well have spit in her face.

"I've been the only mother he's ever known," she said in a rush, frantic to make him understand.

"Those men who were chasing you at the grave-yard were hired by the doctor to find his son?"

She shook her head, knowing she had to trust him

with part of the truth now. "No, Simon isn't Paul's son."

He arched a dark brow.

"Paul is a geneticist. He…he helped me escape with Simon. He wanted me to take him." She knew she was making no sense, but her pulse was clamoring. "I didn't hurt Paul—he was my friend."

His dark gaze wavered, full of more questions.

"That's the truth. I would never hurt anyone. I just want to protect Simon." Desperation turned her voice into a high-pitched squeak. "Please, you have to believe me."

He leaned in so close his nose touched hers. "I don't have to do anything, but *you* have to be honest." His eyes darkened.

"I'm telling the truth now. I just want to protect Simon."

"From whom?"

She curled her fingers into her fists. "I'm not exactly sure."

His glare deepened. "Stop trying to avoid the truth and just spill it."

She examined his face, searching for some sign that he wouldn't betray her if she did confide in him. Paul's warnings about him replayed in her head, yet she had nowhere to turn. "Some people at the research center. They were going to take Simon away. He would never have had a normal life."

"Why would they want to take him away?"

"I don't know everything," she whispered, shivering at the accusations in his eyes. "But I swear I didn't hurt Paul. But they've obviously done something to him.''

"What do you mean?''

"*They* must have hurt or drugged Paul.'' She dropped her head forward, the memory of the doctor's face the last time she'd seen him burning through her.

His gaze locked with hers.

"I swear I'm telling you the truth. I wish I knew everyone involved, but I don't.'' His anger prompted her to rush on. "There's a team of scientists, and I grew suspicious about their work, so I started asking questions. I heard whispers about a secret project that didn't have government clearance. Something to do with the geneticist. Then the doctors started acting funny about Simon. They wouldn't let me take him off the complex, not even to go to Savannah to the park. Then I found out they'd bugged my phone.'' She gasped for breath. "When I asked about adopting Simon, they threatened to fire me. So I started snooping into files and one of the security guards caught me. Then they tried to kill me.''

His questioning gaze wavered.

She spent the next ten minutes answering endless questions about the details of the research center. When he finally seemed content that she actually did work there and had some medical knowledge, his gaze fell to her bruised wrists. "Did Eric know about Simon?''

"Yes.'' She tried to move from behind the wall of his body but he penned her in. "Listen, Cain, I know this sounds crazy, but Paul was a friend of Eric's. He sent me to your brother. He said Eric had helped other women in trouble go underground. He gave me some cash and his car, then he told me to find Eric at the lake.''

She saw the moment the implication sank in.

Cain gripped her wrist. ''So, there was no abusive boyfriend?''

''No. Paul said that Eric worked with a local monastery to help women set up new identities. But when I drove to the monastery, it was closed. Then a man claiming to work with Eric called and told me to meet him at the graveyard. But those other men showed up.''

''The phone call was a setup.''

''I realize that now. They must have gotten my cell phone number from Paul.''

Cain scrubbed a hand over his face. ''If Polenta helped you, why would he give them your number?''

''He wouldn't. Not unless they forced it out of him.'' She sighed. ''They probably drugged him.''

''So, *if* you're telling me the truth, then they might have killed Eric.''

Alanna's throat closed. She could only nod her reply.

SIMON'S CRY BROKE into the tense moment. At Alanna's panicked look, Cain dropped his hands from the wall, temporarily allowing her to leave the imprisonment of his arms. So, the baby wasn't his brother's child. He should feel relieved, yet sadness engulfed him, the loss a palpable ache. The baby wouldn't have taken Eric's place, yet…

His mind spun with questions. He hated the fear

he'd put in her eyes by his brute force, but dammit, she'd lied to him, taken his emotions on a roller-coaster ride. And she might be a criminal.

Was she telling him the truth this time?

He'd heard the news report himself. She was wanted for questioning on kidnapping charges, and had been accused of shooting Simon's father and taking the baby because she couldn't have a child of her own. He'd heard cases where women had breakdowns after learning they couldn't have children and kidnapped babies from nurseries.

That story was much more believable than her bizarre tale.

Yet, in his military and medical background he had heard of other cases where scientists crossed the line and let greed and power rule their decisions. Once he'd even investigated a Middle Eastern terrorist group engineering biochemical weapons. Another team of scientists had infected prisoners with various germs to test their reactions—all in the name of science.

He inched to the bedroom door and watched her through the doorway. She whispered tender loving words to Simon as she changed his diaper.

Truth or not, she obviously loved the baby and Simon loved her. But whether or not she had a right to keep him was another matter.

The monastery was the missing part of the puzzle in Eric's operation. It made sense. He wondered why he hadn't realized the connection before. The priests would definitely help protect abused women and keep their silence.

Had Eric known that Simon wasn't Alanna's baby or had she lied to him as well?

"Come on, honey, let's get you some breakfast." Alanna scooped the baby into her arms, a wary expression on her face as she approached the doorway where he stood. "I'm going to feed Simon, then we'll leave. I don't want you caught in the middle of all this, Cain."

"You're not going anywhere, not unless it's to the authorities."

Her forced smile looked grave. "I can't do that."

The baby batted a hand at her cheek and she caught his fist, then pressed a kiss to it.

"You have to believe me, I'm doing this for Simon."

He didn't question the fact that she loved the baby, just her reasons for running off with him. And unless she gave him some definite proof that the baby was in danger, he had no choice.

Simon didn't belong to her, and he would have to turn her in.

ALANNA PROPPED SIMON in her lap and fed him his morning rice cereal and applesauce, smiling as he cooed and tried to grab the spoon. Twice he helped her move it toward his mouth but missed, and applesauce dribbled down his chin.

At least Cain hadn't phoned the police yet. But that didn't mean he wouldn't. In fact, he had taken her car keys and his with him to the bathroom to keep her from fleeing while he showered.

She tried to force images of him naked, standing

beneath a spray of hot water, from her mind. It had been months since she'd even thought of a man in a sexual way or noticed a man's looks, even longer since she'd met one with as much power and masculinity as Cain Caldwell.

The pain of her husband's betrayal still stung. She had finished school and returned to Macon, Georgia, to work at the local hospital. Donald Jacobs had moved there to take over his grandfather's law practice. They'd met at a fund-raiser for the children's wing and had instantly hit it off, their love of kids drawing them together. After a whirlwind courtship, she had a wedding band and a husband.

Only later, when she'd given him her heart and soul, had she learned that he'd married her simply to get a baby.

His grandfather had stipulated in his will that in order to receive his trust money, Donald had to have a wife and children. It had galled her husband to no end that though he'd become a lawyer he couldn't break the will.

She had been his answer.

But then she'd failed...

Bitter memories of the fertility treatments haunted her; the lengths she'd resorted to in order to conceive before she'd learned the truth, the hurt of knowing she'd done all that because she'd loved Donald when he hadn't really wanted her or a baby at all. All he'd wanted was the money...

Simon pushed away the spoon, and she wiped his chin, then grabbed a bottle and decided to feed him outside by the lake.

Cain suddenly appeared, looking big and brawny. He smelled like soap and aftershave, a deadly combination. He stepped in front of her, blocking the door. "Where do you think you're going?"

"Outside. I thought Simon could use some air." And so could she. She needed to put some space between her and this intimidating man.

"That's not very wise. After all, there are people after you."

Fear pricked at her. "Do you think they followed us here?"

"No, but you can't go wandering off. And until I check out your story, you're not leaving my sight." He gestured toward a tree only a few feet away. "Stay in the thicket there. It's close enough so if someone comes up I can get to you."

Nerves on edge, she glared at him. She had to start thinking like a woman on the run. Like a fugitive. But she didn't like it.

Sunshine bathed the lake, its breathtaking view of woods and nature offering a momentary reprieve from the tension in the cabin. Alanna found a dry patch of grass beneath a sycamore tree, sat down and propped Simon in her lap so he could watch the ripples in the lake water as he drank his bottle. A frog croaked nearby and the wind rustled the trees, lifting her bangs from her eyes.

"Oh, Simon, Mama Alanna's going to take care of you." She smiled at the sound of his suckling, wishing she and Simon were a normal mother and child, out enjoying the day.

But they never would be. There would always be

the threat of someone behind them. Someone trying to take him away.

Simon pushed at the bottle, letting her know he was full, then spit bubbles. She smiled and dabbed at his mouth with a napkin.

"Ma...ma."

Alanna froze, lifting Simon so she could see his face. Simon was only four months old, not old enough to talk. "What did you say, sweetie?"

He laughed, his little mouth parting. "Ma...ma. Ma...ma."

Alanna hugged him to her, her heart squeezing, her mind reeling in disbelief. "Yes, baby, I'm your mama for now." Her voice broke as she glanced back at Cain Caldwell where he stood on the porch.

But for how long?

CAIN SHIFTED uncomfortably and watched Alanna playing with the baby.

What the hell was he doing, harboring a fugitive? Did he really believe her story?

The attack at the graveyard should have shaken her enough to make her realize that she couldn't escape with a young child. He slipped back inside the cabin, keeping an eye on Alanna through the window.

He had to check on the progress in Eric's case and fill his partner in on this latest development. He couldn't jeopardize his reputation as a detective for this woman. Especially when turning her in and finding out the truth about her story might lead him to Eric's killer.

He punched in his partner's number. He had told

Alanna he wouldn't call the police, but he was a cop, sworn to uphold the law.

After all, he didn't owe the woman anything. But he did owe his brother....

Chapter Eight

"Wakefield, what did you find out about the bombing?"

"It was a simple setup, trigger hooked to the ignition. I found evidence of black powder. Any Tom, Dick or Harry could have gotten it at a discount store."

"How about the witness in the Bronsky case? Any word on him?"

"No."

The silence that followed his partner's curt reply seemed deafening. Chances of learning Palmer's whereabouts might have died with Eric. Eric's brutal death would have destroyed any confidence he might have had that the police could protect him.

"Is the search for Palmer active?"

"You know it is. The feds need him or their case is dead in the water."

"Right." Alanna raised Simon above her head and bounced him up and down. The baby cycled his arms and legs.

"How are you holding up?" his partner asked.

"All right." He hesitated, his emotions ping-ponging in his head as Alanna placed Simon on her lap and blew on his stomach. "It's hell just sitting around, though, having to watch the news to find out what's going on in the world."

"Yeah, nothing like getting a jump on crime through the force, is there?"

Cain forced a laugh. "Saw a piece about that baby kidnapping in Savannah. Anything come in about that?"

Wakefield made a clicking sound with his tongue. "Got an APB out on the woman across the state. Freaky stuff happens down there at the research facility."

"What's the latest?"

"Remember the bizarre story about that scientist Wells who was killed? Some of those doctors did an experiment on him and transplanted his memories into a cop's head."

The hair on the back of Cain's neck prickled. He'd been so busy fighting with Eric this past year he hadn't kept up. Nighthawk Island housed confidential cutting-edge research projects for the government, but he had no idea the types of projects they worked on. He assumed it was counterterrorist tactics, biological warfare research, studies relevant since the September eleventh crisis. He'd investigated some mysterious incidents with government projects himself when he was in the Air Force. He'd thought he'd left those horrors behind. Had quit so his life would be simpler, so he'd have more time with Eric.

Alanna's story *could* have credence to it.

Had she stumbled onto some kind of project that involved a baby?

Genetic engineering, cloning, stem cell research, those were hot topics right now.

Cain's gaze shot back to Alanna. She was tickling Simon now, both of them laughing. But he remembered the gaunt shadows beneath her eyes, the fear, the bruises. If there was any possibility that her story might have some truth to it, he couldn't turn her in.

Not yet.

But it was impossible for him to do the legwork and keep an eye on her and the baby at the same time.

"Cain, you there?"

"Yeah, just find that witness the feds lost, and help me nail the bastard who killed my brother."

FOR A FEW MINUTES, Alanna had almost allowed herself to believe that she and Simon were safe, but the sound of leaves crunching under the weight of boots drew her attention back to reality. She scanned the woods, praying the men from the graveyard hadn't found her. Or that Cain had not called his cop buddies to come and take her into custody.

Cain walked toward her, uncertainty still tainting his eyes. She handed Simon the tiny stuffed puppy he liked to cuddle and forced a smile when Cain handed her a cup of coffee. He also had a package of blueberry muffins and offered her one. "Thanks." Her stomach growled and she took one, chewing slowly to stall for time. She inhaled the scent of his soap-cleaned masculine body, which reminded her that he was all male. Big and hard and lean. And sexy as hell with his black hair still damp and combed back from his forehead. Things she shouldn't be noticing.

But he was still angry.

"I...I was afraid you'd called and turned me in."

"I almost did."

His honesty surprised her. Maybe because she'd been lied to by so many men. "Why didn't you?"

"Let's just say the verdict's still out." He wolfed down the muffin, then licked his fingers clean. She averted her gaze, shocked that her body reacted to him. He didn't like her or trust her and she wasn't sure she liked him, either. She certainly didn't trust him.

Or anyone else.

At least not completely. But she did trust that he would keep her and Simon safe from physical harm. That is, if she could convince him to believe her.

"I want the whole story."

Their gazes locked. "I told you—"

"You told me bits and pieces. I want it from beginning to end. How you came to care for Simon. Everything you know about this geneticist and his work at the research center. Why you ran."

She nodded, although the research involving Simon still had gaping holes that she had yet to fill in. Simon tried to stuff the puppy's ear in his mouth, so she handed him a plastic teething ring to chew on instead. "I heard about innovative fertility treatments at CIRP—"

"CIRP?"

"The Coastal Island Research Park on Catcall Island near Savannah. They have facilities on Catcall, more planned on Whistlestop Island, and some highly classified government projects out on Nighthawk Island.''

He gestured for her to continue, his gaze softening when he looked at Simon gumming the teething toy.

''Anyway, I worked as a nurse at the hospital in Macon and had heard of the facility, so I went there for fertility treatments.''

''They weren't successful?''

She had to look away. The painful memories taunted her. ''No.''

He leaned back against the tree, studying her. ''Go on.''

''I met Dr. Polenta there. He was consulting on another case. We struck up a conversation in the elevator.''

''Was that when you started taking care of Simon?''

''No.'' The memory of leaving the clinic in defeat settled around her. She remembered the fight with her ex-husband, his callous remarks. Their divorce. ''I returned to Macon, and my marriage ended.''

''Your husband left you because you couldn't have a baby?''

Alanna nodded, her throat too thick to speak.

''Jerk.''

She bit down on her lip but let his comment slide, although his assessment soothed her somewhat. All this time she'd blamed herself, had told herself Donald had every right to be disappointed in her, yet she'd secretly hoped that if he'd loved her, he would understand and want her anyway. Of course, he hadn't loved her at all....

"What happened after that, Alanna?"

His voice had lowered now, his tone less harsh. She took a deep breath. "About three months later, Paul— Dr. Polenta—called and asked me if I'd consider becoming a private nurse. He said a baby had been born premature and he needed special care." That phone call had been a lifesaver. Or so she'd thought at the time. "It seemed like the perfect answer for me. I needed to get out of Macon, away from my ex. And...I thought my prayers had been answered. I was all alone, and so was this helpless little baby. He needed me."

A long silence descended between them. Her comment could provide the motivation to frame her as a kidnapper.

"What about his birth mother and father? Where did they fit into the picture?"

She stroked Simon's soft cheek as he slowly nodded off to sleep. "Dr. Polenta told me that Simon's mother abandoned him. As a preemie, Simon had complications that freaked her out. She said she couldn't afford to take care of a sick child." Alanna paused, steadying her voice, knowing that her anger at the woman had filtered through. "So, I went to Catcall Island. I took care of Simon in the hospital for the first two weeks, then brought him home."

"He lived with you?"

"Yes, the research facility built several cabins on their grounds. We lived in one of them."

"Why wasn't Simon turned over to the mother's nearest relatives or to the state?"

"I asked Paul the same question," Alanna said, remembering the awkward conversation. "He claimed the mother was an orphan herself and had no family. That was one reason she wanted a child of her own." A breeze ruffled the leaves, and she tucked another blanket over Simon.

"But she signed away her rights?"

Alanna nodded.

"What about the state?"

"Paul said the head of the clinic was working with the state, but Simon needed special monitoring in the beginning, and they couldn't place him until they resolved his health issues."

"What kinds of problems did he have?"

"Nothing visible. But his birth weight was low, and his lungs weren't completely developed. Dr. Polenta said he might have a gene abnormality and needed further testing."

Cain folded his arms across his chest. "How much do you know about Polenta's work?"

Alanna shrugged. "He focuses on using genetic engineering to develop cancer and AIDS vaccines."

"You're sure Polenta isn't Simon's father?"

Alanna squeezed the puppy to her chest. "I suppose it's possible he was the sperm donor, but if he was, he never told me."

"Then you two were close?"

Alanna hesitated. "We were friends. He enjoyed visiting Simon." And she'd sensed he enjoyed seeing her, too, but she'd been so broken up over her divorce that she hadn't encouraged him.

Now he was lying comatose in a hospital, possibly dying. All because he'd helped her escape with Simon. He had wanted to save Simon, too, she reminded herself.

She couldn't let his sacrifice go for nothing.

CAIN FOCUSED on Alanna, determined to read every nuance of her body language for lies, but so far, her story sounded rational. "So, you took care of Simon while the doctors continued to run tests?"

"Yes." Alanna thought back to that Monday two weeks ago. "Finally I approached Paul about adopting Simon. I figured he might have an in with Dr. Peterson, the head of the fertility clinic."

"What did he say?"

"He got really nervous and started avoiding me. He even suggested that if I pushed the matter or asked too many questions about Simon, I would lose my job. Then I saw Paul and Peterson having several hushed conversations and heard tidbits of talk about the tests Britain was doing with embryo cloning to create stem cells. That's when I started wondering if everything they'd told me was true."

Simon squirmed as he slept, and Alanna patted his back. "What exactly was it that bothered you?"

"By then, Simon was starting to gain weight and seemed healthy. I didn't understand why they wouldn't let me adopt him. Paul became angry with me, and Peterson, the head of the fertility clinic, gave me a flat-out no."

"That does seem odd. It's unusual for a hospital to keep an infant so long."

"Exactly. It was almost as if they felt Simon belonged to them. And I heard they were petitioning the government for approval for embryo cloning themselves."

"You said earlier that you were snooping around in the files?"

Alanna nodded. "Yes, I overheard Peterson and Dr. Forrester, the OB-GYN who delivered Simon, talking about Simon's mother."

"And?"

"They made it sound as if she'd died during childbirth, but Paul had told me she'd abandoned him."

"Hmm."

Alanna hugged her arms around herself and turned her face upward toward the sun as if she needed its warmth. Sunshine splintered through the trees. At least she looked more rested today, the purple bruises beneath her eyes beginning to fade. "I wanted to find out more, so I went snooping in Dr. Peterson's office. I found Simon's medical records in his computer, but they were password protected."

"Is that unusual?"

Alanna shivered again. "For a normal pregnancy, yes. But that wasn't the strangest part."

"What?"

"His file was listed as Project Simon."

"DID YOU FIND HER?"

"Not yet."

His boss released a string of expletives that singed

his ear through the phone. He'd been pissed the night before when he'd had to report that they'd lost the Hayes broad at the graveyard. Now he'd moved past pissed into livid.

"Why the hell not?"

"Atlanta's a big area. We will find her, though." And that creep who'd shot at them. Caldwell's brother.

"Keep looking. Meanwhile, we've gone to Plan B. Polenta went public."

"I saw the report on the news this morning. What if the police pick her up and she squeals?"

"She doesn't know enough to give them anything concrete. Besides, she's on the defensive now. The last thing she wants is to end up in jail and lose Simon to the authorities." He coughed into the phone. "Now, find Simon and bring him back to me."

"What do I do if the woman is with Caldwell?"

"Kill them both. We don't want any loose ends that might come back to haunt us."

Chapter Nine

Project Simon?

Cain's skin crawled—could that innocent little baby be part of a cloning experiment? He was fairly certain American scientists weren't able to clone humans yet, although they were close. Animals were a different story. The University of Georgia led the field in cloning cattle. Mice, cats, sheep and pigs had also been successfully cloned, though problems still existed.

Alanna studied him warily as if she anticipated he might bolt and phone the authorities any second.

He still didn't know why he hadn't. Maybe he felt he owed Eric something for all the times he hadn't supported him in his efforts to help troubled women. Maybe he owed his own mother for not saving her from their abusive father.

Maybe he just found Alanna so damn appealing and, if her story were true, downright *courageous,* that he couldn't stand to see the baby she loved so much torn from her arms.

But if her story weren't true...well, hell, at least

she wouldn't harm Simon, not like those thugs who'd come after her with guns. He sure as hell didn't want them to get their hands on the baby. Waiting a little longer before letting the authorities know Alanna's whereabouts wouldn't hurt anything. But he absolutely wouldn't let her out of his sight.

If Simon was the result of a secret study, it made sense that the scientists would want to monitor him. But would scientists try to shoot Alanna in order to get him back? Would Simon's own father hire someone to find them? Would they kill Eric to prevent him from helping her?

Cain shoved his hands through his hair, unable to fathom why he almost believed Alanna's story.

A baby's life depended on the choices he made right now.

"I have a friend in the FBI—"

"No, Cain, you can't tell anyone." Alanna grabbed his hand, her slender fingers curling over his larger ones.

"He can help me check out the research center. If what you told me is true, I have to know what kind of project we're talking about so we know how to proceed."

Panic flared in Alanna's huge eyes. "You believe me?"

"I'm not sure what I believe, but I will find out the truth. If Eric died because of Simon, I want to know."

"You'd turn him in to get revenge?"

Anger sharpened his voice. "That's not what I meant. I just want the truth." He stood, facing the lake, a thousand emotions warring in his head. "I'm a cop, Alanna. I've always lived by the law. That's who I am."

Her shaky breathing filled the silence. "If you contact the police and tell them about Simon, they'll give him back to those doctors who will put him in a lab. He'll never have a normal life."

"If evidence proves he's not Polenta's son, and that he has no parents, the state will find him a home." He lowered his eyes, stared at his boots. "Maybe you can adopt him, then."

"You don't understand." Alanna stood and gripped his arm, forcing him to look at her. "The people at CIRP will never let that happen."

"If he is different—some kind of project—and the police find that's true, the media will make the public aware, then the researchers will be held accountable."

Her fingers dug into his arm, her voice rising near hysteria. "But if Simon is a part of a project and the press get wind of it, they'll turn his life into a nightmare. That's the reason I didn't go to them when I left with Simon in the first place."

In spite of his reservations, Cain placed a comforting hand over Alanna's. She was right. But the question remained—what exactly was Project Simon?

And was Simon's mother dead or alive?

ALANNA HAD TO THINK of a plan.

Thankfully, she'd bought herself some time with Cain, but she didn't trust that he still wouldn't turn her in.

When Simon had awakened, they called a truce.

She fed the baby while Cain fixed them sandwiches and they ate by the lake. Simon giggled and looked at the rippling water as if he recognized the peace and beauty of it. Once again Alanna had wondered if he had some special sense. Could his early language development be related to the research?

Finally the temperature started to drop and they went inside. Cain turned sullen again and seemed obsessed with researching CIRP on his computer. Simon fell asleep in her arms.

While Simon napped, she borrowed Cain's shower, contemplating her next step. If Eric had used a monastery to help abused women go underground, perhaps she'd gone to the wrong one. There were others listed in the phone book in a different area. She'd try every one of them until she could find someone who had known him and would help her.

As much as she wanted to believe that Cain was her savior, she knew better than to count on him. Or most other men. But a priest might just be the answer.

CAIN TRIED TO IGNORE the reaction his body had when he heard Alanna in his shower, the thoughts of her delicate body covered in soapy bubbles, water licking and trickling over skin that had seen more brutality than a fragile woman like her deserved. Or was she fragile?

Could she be a cunning liar trying to manipulate him into believing her story?

Other women had tried to do so in the past.

But none of them had affected him the way Alanna did.

Shaking off the lingering memory of her fingers digging into his arm, he downloaded everything he could find on CIRP, hoping to gain some insight on the fertility clinic and the genetics department. And Project Simon.

Several minutes later, he scrolled over the newspaper clippings detailing events of the last year and a half.

The latest story covered the experimental memory transplant his partner had mentioned earlier. A local Savannah cop, Clayton Fox, had been investigating the research park and had gone to meet one of the scientists, a man named Tom Wells. Wells had apparently grown a conscience over a project he'd undertaken and had decided to give Fox the inside scoop, but Wells had been killed. Hoping to cover their tracks, the scientists decided to get rid of Fox by erasing his memory and replacing it with memory cells from Tom Wells. They had hoped to isolate the memory cells and keep Wells's knowledge of his work but hadn't counted on the fact that Fox might also gain Wells's personal memories. The experiment had been a disaster in the minds of the researchers and had led to several arrests.

Cain stood and poured himself another cup of coffee, shaking his head. Good God, what were those researchers thinking? Playing with people's lives like that, transferring memories from one man to another.

His curiosity piqued, he sat back down and searched for more.

Arnold Hughes, the former CEO and a co-founder of the Coastal Island Research Park had supposedly died when his boat exploded following the death of his partner, Sol Santenelli. But if Hughes's body hadn't been recovered, he could still be alive. Apparently he was ruthless—he'd even tried to kill Santenelli's goddaughter.

Cain scratched his head. Denise Harley, a research scientist at CIRP, had been working on a project to alter cognitive growth through gene therapy. Her research was inconclusive. She destroyed the files because the genetic engineering was faulty and posed ethical questions which could be even more controversial if they fell into the wrong hands.

Cain glanced toward the bedroom. Could Simon be the product of a similar research experiment?

The shower water went silent just as the phone rang.

"Caldwell here."

"It's Wakefield."

His adrenaline shot up. "What's going on?"

"Atlanta P.D. had a John Doe burn victim turn up at Grady Hospital. Burned so badly they haven't been able to ID him, but the feds are hoping he's their witness, Palmer."

That would be a relief. "Doing DNA?"

"Yeah, but it'll take time."

"I know. Any news on the Banks murder? They found his killer?" Then Eric would be off the hook for that one.

"Afraid not." Silence ticked between them.

Cain gritted his teeth. His partner was holding back. "What else, Wakefield?"

"So far, all trails lead back to your brother."

Cain hissed, "What trails?"

"APD found Eric's fingerprints on the door inside Banks's apartment."

"He didn't do it," Cain insisted. "My brother might have been a vigilante, and he may have crossed the line a few times, but he wasn't a murderer."

"Listen, Cain, it could have been self-defense."

"No." Cain dropped his head into his hands. "Has the murder weapon been recovered?"

"No. Coroner said the stab wounds look like they're from a kitchen knife. Probably took it with him and threw it out."

"Dammit, Wakefield, it wasn't Eric."

"I'm just keeping you updated."

Cain clenched his hands into fists. "Thanks. Have Wade and Pirkle dug anything up on the people after Palmer?"

"Feds aren't offering up any information."

That didn't surprise him. They certainly wouldn't care about Eric's death, especially if they thought he'd interfered with their case.

"Keep me posted." His partner agreed and Cain hung up, automatically digging Eric's gold cross from his pocket. Clutching the cross in his fingers, he removed the photo of him and Eric from his wallet. Unfortunately he and Eric had grown up to see more bad than good, Eric with his work and Cain with the police force.

Was Alanna part of that good?

ALANNA STOOD in the middle of the doorway, her heart breaking at the pain in Cain's face. She ached to go to him and offer him comfort, but she had no right.

Not if she had caused his brother's death.

But she couldn't stand still and do nothing.

She moved toward him slowly, the object he held in his hand glittering in the afternoon sunlight streaming through the room. He was also looking at a photograph. Her footsteps clicked in the silence and he turned to look at her, the emotions in his dark eyes so intense her breath caught.

Then she glimpsed the photograph and recognized a younger Cain and another man who resembled him. "Is that your brother?"

He nodded and pushed the picture toward her. "A couple of years ago."

She took the picture and studied the men, her pulse throbbing. Eric stood about an inch shorter than Cain, his hair a fraction of a shade lighter, and he had the same deep sadness in his eyes. But he also had an angry glint to his jaw that spelled attitude and defiance.

"Were you close?"

"Sort of." His fingers tightened around the object in his hand, which she recognized as a gold cross.

"Did the cross belong to Eric?"

He nodded. "My partner found it beside the car after the fire. My mother gave it to Eric on his thirteenth birthday. He never took it off."

"I'm so sorry, Cain. How's your mother taking the news about Eric?"

A hardness settled onto his face, masking his emotions. "My mother's dead. She killed herself. Old man left after that. Guess he figured he'd lost his punching bag.''

Alanna winced at the bitterness in his voice.

''What about you, Alanna?'' Their fingers brushed as she handed him back the photograph, a spark of electricity rippling between them. She wanted to reach out and comfort him, take away that bitterness. His husky voice washed over her. ''Don't you have family out there somewhere wondering where you are?''

''I guess we're both pretty much alone.'' She dropped her hand, desperately wishing to hide the fact that he affected her. ''My parents died in a car crash when I was twelve. My grandmother raised me.''

''Is she gone, too?''

''She has Alzheimer's. She's in a nursing home now.'' His look of sympathy unnerved her. ''Sometimes she recognizes me, some days not.''

''That's tough.''

Alanna shrugged. At first, she'd been devastated but she'd soon learned to live alone. Then she'd met and married Donald and thought her life was going to be a fairy tale. Instead it had been a nightmare.

Cain must have sensed her agony because he brought a hand up and gently brushed a water droplet from her cheek. She'd towel-dried her short hair; it had been so long since she'd worried about her looks that she hadn't given it a second thought.

Now she wondered what Cain thought. Did he find her unattractive? Did he see her inability to have a child as a defect like her ex-husband had?

''In some ways I guess we are alike,'' he said in a

quiet voice. He brushed his knuckles gently across her bruised cheek. ''Who did this to you?''

''The guards who held me captive after they found me snooping around,'' she said in a shaky voice. ''One of them seemed to take pleasure in his job.''

A muscle ticked in his jaw and she remembered his declaration about his father.

''You said they tried to kill you?''

''Yes.'' She could feel his breath on her face. ''The guards locked me in a lab storage room. Paul rescued me just before the building blew up.''

''There was a bomb?''

''I guess so, the building exploded.''

''A bomb blew up Eric's car, too.''

Alanna froze. She knew exactly what Cain was thinking. ''I'm s-so sorry, Cain. I never meant to get anyone else hurt or involved.''

ALANNA'S GUILT-STRICKEN expression forced Cain's anger at bay. If she was telling the truth, then she wasn't at fault, but the bastards who had started this whole sordid chain of events had to be punished.

And if Eric had died because of his commitment to help Alanna and baby Simon, he owed it to his brother to protect them.

Only he was starting to think of Alanna as more than a job.

Her eyes seemed huge in her pale face, her small pink lips quivering with sadness. Yet, when he'd touched her cheek, he'd felt a shiver of awareness course through her that affected him.

Unable to stop himself, he tilted her chin up with

his hand, lowered his mouth and brushed his lips across hers. He only wanted to offer her comfort.

Or maybe he wanted it for himself....

"YOU FOUND CALDWELL?"

He stretched out his legs, twisting a toothpick in his mouth as his partner tossed his fishing line over the side. "I'm right outside his cabin, in a fishing boat on the lake."

"I didn't send you on a damn vacation."

"It's the best place to watch the cabin. You don't want us to get spotted stalking a cop, do you?"

"No." His boss grunted, the hiss of his breath cutting over the telephone line. "Just hurry up and bring the baby back to me. The more time she has, the more likely she'll talk to someone. In fact, I'm putting a man at the nursing home where the grandmother is just in case she shows up there."

He bristled. His boss didn't trust him to do the job.

They wouldn't need anyone at the nursing home; he'd make sure of that. "We'll make our move tonight." He glanced at the dark, murky water.

It was the perfect burial spot for the cop and the woman.

Chapter Ten

Alanna sank into Cain's arms, the touch of his mouth on hers irresistible. It had been so long since anyone had offered her comfort, much less tenderness, that tears threatened to spill from her eyes. Other emotions welled inside her, too.

Cain pulled her against the hard wall of his body, his hands slipping into her hair. He nibbled at her lips, then slid his tongue inside her mouth. She moaned softly and clung to the corded muscles in his arms, her heart fluttering with feelings left dormant for so long she'd forgotten she even possessed them.

Surrendering to the need building within her, she ran her hand down his back. The low sound that rumbled from his throat sent warmth pooling inside her. Deepening the kiss, he trailed his fingers over her shoulders, beside her breasts, then down her waist, where he let them linger momentarily before he cupped her buttocks and rocked her closer to him. Desire surged through her, her nipples hardening to peaks as his chest crushed her sensitive breasts. His sex hardened and pulsed against her stomach, the realization that his hunger for her was real igniting her senses to a fever pitch.

Simon's cry tore through the passion engulfing Alanna, the reality of their situation splintering the hunger. She pulled away at the same time he did, his face a mask of ironclad control, although the rapid rise and fall of his chest belied his calm.

He had wanted her physically.

But she could read the doubts and uncertainty in his eyes.

"I'm sorry. That was a mistake." He shoved a hand through his hair, backing away, his gaze aimed toward the bedroom where Simon's cry escalated. Alanna saw the picture of his brother on the table as she scrambled away, and remembered their earlier conversation.

They both thought his brother might have been killed because of her and Simon. Even if Cain didn't blame her for Eric's death, he wanted to catch the killer. Just how far would he go?

Would he seduce her to get her to confide in him? Would he use her and Simon to catch his brother's killer?

THE SHARP END of Eric's cross cut into Cain's fingers, reminding him of all the reasons he shouldn't get involved with Alanna.

Still his body pulsed with need, the hunger so strong he'd almost reached out and pulled her back into his arms instead of letting her go.

What the hell was wrong with him?

He never allowed his emotions to interfere with his

job. No shades of gray for him, only black-and-white. But black-and-white urged him to call the feds and turn Alanna and the baby over to them.

And after that kiss, he had no intention of doing that.

But he would dig deeper and find the truth.

Alanna returned seconds later with Simon snuggled to her, the little boy's face aglow with adoration as she cooed baby talk to him. The tension in Cain's body slowly dissipated at the sight of her smile. The rarity transformed her into an elegant beauty.

It was enough to make a man forget his mission.

But not the fact that he'd just lost his brother.

Or maybe his grief had thrust him into a pit of despair, fueling his hunger more. He needed comfort to ease the hollow pain inside him and she just happened to be available.

He knew the dangers in letting a pair of pretty blue eyes lead him astray. But still he wanted her.

Alanna walked Simon to the window and propped him in her arms so he could see outside into the darkness. "It's nighttime now, Simon," she whispered. "See that yellow sliver in the sky. That's the moon."

Cain grinned as memories of his mother surfaced, the old rhyme about seeing the moon playing over in his head. She used to tuck him and Eric in bed and tickle them, then sing them to sleep.

Those sweet, happy memories had gotten lost in the grief he'd experienced after her suicide.

He walked to the window and stood beside Alanna, taking in the bond between her and Simon. Was she a desperate woman who'd kidnapped him or a courageous one who'd saved him from spending his life under scientific scrutiny?

Either way, he had to know. And he had to figure out if someone was still after her and Simon. If so, they wouldn't be safe until things were resolved.

"Did Polenta ever mention Denise Harley's research?"

Alanna frowned and rocked Simon back and forth. "No. I read something about it, though. Apparently she'd been experimenting with gene therapy to alter intelligence."

"Trying to create the super human, huh?"

"I don't think so. I got the impression from some of the other doctors at the center that she intended to use it to help prevent mental defects in infants at risk."

"But someone else had other ideas?"

Alanna nodded. "I heard that was the reason she destroyed her files."

"What if the files weren't destroyed? What if someone resurrected her work and took it a step further?"

Alanna's gaze swung to his. "You mean with Simon?"

"I'm just speculating." Cain shrugged. "But it's worth checking out."

She nodded, the faint despair in her eyes replaced with wariness. And the memory of that kiss.

He swallowed and ignored the simmering attraction, afraid he'd get burned if he touched her again. Afraid he wouldn't be able to stop until he made love to her. "Did Polenta tell you Simon's mother's name?"

She shook her head. "I was trying to access his birth records when the guards caught me."

"Did the doctors ever mention that Simon had special needs?"

"No. But just before I left with Simon, Polenta warned me not to go to the press. He said they'd ruin Simon's life. And when I was tied up, I heard another man mention that the Russians wanted their research."

Cain stewed over the information. "And you don't know if Simon's mother is dead or alive."

"No."

"If the doctors wanted to keep Simon to themselves, then they wouldn't want the mother around."

"What?"

"Say that Simon is a product of some kind of research. Maybe the mother was an innocent chosen to carry the fetus and had no idea they were conducting an experiment on her baby, or she could have been a paid surrogate."

Alanna nodded.

"Then Simon is born and the scientists want him kept near the lab so they can monitor him. There are several possibilities. One, if she was a paid surrogate, she might have taken the money and run. Two, she could have died accidentally in childbirth. Or..."

"Or what?"

"Or the scientists could have killed the mother to protect the project."

Alanna's legs wavered and Cain steadied her.

"It's also possible that the mother might have abandoned Simon, or they could have lied to her and told her the baby had died. Then she might not know Simon is even alive."

ALANNA COULDN'T BELIEVE what Cain was suggesting. Yet, she knew someone from the center had tried to kill her, so the idea that they might kill Simon's mother and cover it up, or lie to her about his birth wasn't so farfetched.

"Alanna, I'm sorry." Cain's low voice sounded soothing, but nothing could alleviate the fear pounding in her head. "I know you don't want to think about the possibility and it may not be true—"

Alanna met his worried gaze directly. "If Simon's mother didn't abandon him, if she finds out he's alive, she might want to claim him."

"There are things we can do to find out." He placed a comforting hand on her shoulder. "I'll check into records. See what I can dig up."

Alanna nodded, too distraught to reply. Simon tugged at her shirt and she glanced down into his trusting face. She loved him as if he was her own. But did he have a mother out there somewhere looking for him? A mother that had not willingly abandoned him and never intended to let him go?

She couldn't shake her anxiety as she went through the motions of feeding Simon and forcing down a few bites of the dinner Cain had prepared. Finally she gave up and laid down her fork.

"You didn't eat much."

Alanna shrugged.

"I know I'm no cook, but—"

"It's not the food, Cain." The prepackaged spa-ghetti sauce had been fine.

His silent perusal made her squirm. He understood. Maybe too much.

Her earlier plan to call the monasteries and find someone to help her escape came rushing back. But if Simon did have a mother somewhere who wanted him, could Alanna live with herself if she went into hiding?

There's no proof his mother is alive or that she didn't abandon him.

"Mama. Mama." Simon babbled from the quilt on the floor and Cain surprised her by standing. "I'll get him. You look exhausted."

Alanna ran a finger down the glass of tea, wiping away the condensation. Cain knelt and scooped Simon up, his big body even more massive with the baby cradled in his arms. Simon quieted instantly, his innocent gaze surveying Cain's features as if deciding whether or not to trust him.

Alanna still hadn't decided herself.

She certainly didn't trust herself with him.

Suddenly nervous, she began to clear the dishes.

"You don't have to do that. I can get it later."

"It's all right." She forced a smile she didn't feel and tried not to watch Cain cradle Simon in his arms. The entire scene felt too domestic, too much like the fairy-tale life she'd dreamed about. Sharing a house, dinner, a baby. And later, a bed...

But their situation was only temporary and she had

to remember that. She would not share her bed
with Cain.

In fact, she'd never have a permanent relationship
with Cain. They would both always know that her
appearance in his life had meant his brother's death.

"Hey, buddy," Cain said.

Cain carried Simon to the door, then stepped outside. "Let's see if we hear the frogs."

Alanna smiled, although an emptiness swelled inside her when they disappeared out the door. She
watched him with Simon as she loaded the dishes into
the dishwasher and scrubbed the spaghetti pot. When
she'd finally finished, she headed outside to join them.

Simon's gurgling and Cain's gruff voice echoed
through the wind as Cain pointed out the night sounds
and the constellations in the sky. Alanna turned her
head upward and searched for the brightest star she
could find. But even as she closed her eyes and made
a wish, she doubted it would come true.

She had learned long ago that it was always calm-
est before the storm. And with the mystery surrounding Simon and all the questions about his birth and
his mother, a major one was brewing on the horizon.

Finally they walked side by side on the path back
to the house. Shadows flickered from the leaves
above, the moon peeking through the bare limbs.
Alanna reached for Simon. "I should give him a bath
before his next bottle. Then he'll probably go down
for the night."

Cain nodded. Their fingers brushed as he placed
Simon into her arms and heat spiraled through her.

Shaken already by the earlier kiss, she ignored the sensations pulling at her and hurried inside.

An hour later, she tucked Simon into bed and curled up beside him. But even though the baby slept peacefully beside her, sleep eluded her, and she stared into the darkness, feeling cold and alone.

She still might lose Simon.

THROUGH THE PAPER-THIN WALLS, Cain heard Alanna tossing and turning in the other room and grimaced. Part of him wanted to tiptoe inside and comfort her, assure her that everything would be all right, that Simon was hers forever. But he couldn't.

Because those promises might be lies.

His hand gripped the phone, his mind warring over how to handle the situation. He had to know the truth, and the only way to accomplish that was to investigate the research center. Fear had laced Alanna's voice when she'd begged him not to call the FBI or the police, but he couldn't play bodyguard and do all the footwork himself. He had to get in touch with somebody who might have a contact in the medical world. He had to trust someone. Luke Devlin's name immediately came to mind. His buddy worked for a special unit of the FBI that focused on government projects. Cain had saved his life once; now he'd call in the favor.

He punched in the number. The phone rang four times, then the standard recorded message kicked on. "Luke, this is Cain Caldwell. Give me a call—it's urgent." He recited his home number, then his cell, and hung up, his nerves on edge.

Hoping Luke wasn't out of reach, and would call him back that night, he logged on to the computer and pulled up the articles he'd already downloaded about the Coastal Island Research Park. He spent the next hour reading about the various research companies and projects that had become public knowledge.

He couldn't access the confidential files, and wondered if he'd missed something the first go-around. He even checked out the Web site, studied the layout of the buildings and the center, noting the smaller facilities on Whistlestop Island and the more mysterious facility on Nighthawk Island. The cabins Alanna had told him about on Catcall Island were spread out across the facility just as she'd described.

Was she telling the truth about everything else, too?

Cain paced to the window and stared out at the endless dark night. The dim glow of a cigarette lit the inky distance, coming from the nearby cove. Probably that fisherman he'd spotted earlier. The man had been out there all day—should he check him out?

The phone suddenly trilled, startling him from his anxious thoughts and he crossed the room and grabbed it. "Caldwell here."

"Hey, it's Luke." His old friend hesitated, his voice low. "Sorry to hear about your brother, man."

Cain grimaced. "Thanks."

"You said it was urgent?"

"Yeah, I have a favor to ask, but it has to be kept confidential."

"Sounds serious."

"It is. And I mean it, Luke. This can't go any further than you. No one at the agency can know you're checking into this.''

''What's going on, Cain?''

''I need you to dig up all the information you can find on the Coastal Island Research Park. See if there are any government projects under investigation, what the latest controversial research is all about. Focus on gene therapy and a Dr. Paul Polenta.''

''The doctor with the missing baby? Why the sudden interest?''

''Let's just say it might lead back to Eric's killer.''

''I don't understand.''

''I can't explain everything right now, but most importantly, see what you can find on a project entitled Project Simon.''

''Wait a minute, isn't that the missing baby's name?''

''Yeah.''

Indecision laced Luke's voice. ''You can't give me any more than that?''

''I'm afraid not.'' Cain glanced at the bedroom where Simon and Alanna slept. Guilt weighed on his conscience for going against her wishes and consulting his friend. But he couldn't continue hiding her whereabouts without a thorough understanding of the case.

He thanked Luke, then hung up and went back to the computer, logging on to the central database at the police department. First he checked for reports on any recent explosions on Catcall Island. An empty warehouse had burned, supposedly due to a chemical fire.

Was that the warehouse where they'd held Alanna?

He accessed birth records, searching for a birth certificate filed on baby Simon. Odd, he found no baby-boy listing by the name of Simon or any other name on or around the date Alanna said Simon was born.

Curiosity prickled at him. On the off chance that Simon's mother might have died during childbirth, he scrolled through a listing of death certificates from the same date but found nothing.

Weary, he walked back to the door and scanned the lake for the fisherman but didn't see him, so he finally forced himself to go to bed. Not that he would sleep with Alanna next door and his brother gone. And so many unanswered questions.

Why hadn't the doctors filed a birth certificate on Simon? It was almost as if they didn't want anyone to know he existed.

And why was he putting himself and his career on the line for this woman?

Because she was the only person he'd connected with besides Eric and his partner?

He had never bucked the system, had thrived on building a stable life, yet now he was going against everything ingrained in him to help Alanna. What would happen if he took the chance and things backfired in his face?

He'd already lost his brother. Without his job, what would he have left?

PHYLLIS SLUMPED in her car and lit a cigarette, clutching the downy-soft baby blanket to her heart as she stared at the lights in the cabin where her baby slept. Darkness slowly descended over the lake, robbing the sky of its cheerful glow, the night sounds of crickets and frogs and an owl's low hoot mingling with the rippling water splashing against the bank. A lone fisherman sat in a nearby cove, a small lantern propped beside him, occasionally casting looks at Caldwell's cabin as if he, too, had some stake on the inhabitants.

She took a long, slow drag of the cigarette, flicked her ashes in the near-empty coffee cup, and pressed the blanket against her cheek. The baby items she'd bought lay in the back seat, the diapers were in the trunk, and the papers…well, she had almost everything she needed to prove that Simon belonged to her. Not quite, but almost… "It won't be long, Simon. It won't be long until I hold you in my arms."

Damn Alanna Hayes for hooking up with this cop. He was a major glitch in her well-laid plans.

So far, Alanna must have kept her mouth shut. No police or feds had shown up. No press. Maybe Alanna was smarter than she'd given her credit.

Still, she wasn't smart enough to outrun her. Or to keep Simon from her forever.

Phyllis rocked back and forth, stroking the blanket to her cheek while she sang the lullaby she would sing to Simon, "Hush little baby, don't say a word…"

Sometime soon, she would have the birth certificate and everything else she needed to claim Simon. Caldwell would have to leave Alanna and the baby alone sometime.

Then she would make her move.

And Simon would finally be with her, where he belonged.

SIMON WAS LOCKED *in a lab. Confined to the sterile atmosphere and constant company of the scientists who monitored his every movement.*

No. She couldn't let that happen. She and Simon escaped but people followed them. Shooting at them. She ran through the woods. Bullets pinged past her head. She fell to the ground, covering Simon. Smoke curled above them.

Then someone tried to take him. They pried him from her arms.

SMOKE CURLED in a fog above her, and the smell of burning wood filled the room. She'd been dreaming. Alanna opened her eyes. No! She wasn't in the woods.

The smoke was real. Fire blazed beyond the doorway. Wood splintered and popped. She had to get Simon and get out of there.

She tried to scream but the sound died as a shadowy figure leaned over and grabbed her by the throat.

Chapter Eleven

Cain jerked upright, his senses reeling at the smell of smoke. He raced to the hallway but stopped cold when he saw his den ablaze, the path to the room where Alanna and Simon slept in flames. Wood hissed and popped. Flames licked the floor, slowly building from the front doorway to the bedroom. The fire had been deliberately set. He smelled gasoline and saw the red-hot blaze streaking in a line from the doorway.

"Alanna!" He ran back to his bedroom, grabbed a quilt and wrapped it around himself, then raced through the blaze and slammed his body into the doorway. The door sprang open and he glimpsed a shadowy figure holding Alanna in a choking grip. Her strangled scream tore through the air just as Cain lunged forward. Alanna was kicking the man with her feet and slamming her fists wildly. Fury surged inside Cain, spiking his adrenaline. With one quick motion, he grabbed the hulking man and threw him to the floor. The beefy attacker's head slammed against the corner of the end table, his head lolled back and he collapsed.

Cain didn't have time to fool with him. "Come on, let's get out of here—this old place will go up in seconds."

Alanna nodded, pushing hair from her forehead as she scooped Simon into her arms. Simon's shrill cry pierced the air. The flames clawed at the floor inside the room now, hissing and chewing the faded carpet. Smoke curled like a snake sucking oxygen from the air. He wrapped the quilt around his hand, and rammed his fist through the window, sending glass slivers flying.

"Help!" Simon cried. Smoke choked them all. Alanna coughed, pulled Simon's blanket over his face and tried to soothe him.

"You go first." He eased Simon into his arms and helped her crawl through the window, then handed the baby to her and dove headfirst to the ground just as the flames engulfed the bed behind them.

ALANNA CLUTCHED Simon to her chest and slid down onto the ground, watching in horror as fire swallowed the bedroom where she and Simon had just been sleeping. Dear God, they had both almost died. If it hadn't been for Cain…

Had Simon said *help?* Or had she misunderstood in the tumult of the fire?

"Are you all right?" Cain cupped her face in his hands and searched her eyes.

Alanna nodded. "I can't believe this is happening."

"I know." He kissed her quickly on the mouth. "I have to go back in and see if I can save that thug."

"No." Alanna reached for him, but he was already running around to the front side of the house. Fear gripped her. She cradled Simon to her, backed away from the scalding heat, then ran to the front to watch for Cain. But fire engulfed the wooden cabin. In the background, her mind registered the sound of a motor mingled with the hissing fire, and a boat puttering away in the distance.

Her heart thumped wildly as she counted the seconds, praying Cain would make it out alive. Seconds later, he emerged, tossing Simon's bag on the ground and carrying his laptop and cell phone. Sweat poured off his face as he dialed 911.

In spite of the heat from the flames, Alanna shivered as she remembered the intruder in her bedroom.

"Did you find him?"

His expression looked grave as he shook his head. "Too late. He's dead."

He came to her then and she fell into his arms, the strength in his embrace a balm to her trembling soul. Simon whimpered and Cain curled a hand over his head, shushing him with sweet words of comfort as they clung together.

TERROR TIGHTENED Phyllis's muscles as she stared at the burning house.

Those idiots! She had almost lost Simon. If she'd had a gun, she would have shot the thug herself when he'd set the fire. But from her vantage point down the dirt road she hadn't seen him go inside.

She saw the fire now, had first spotted the smoke spiraling through the trees and drifting toward the black sky from her car. The bright flicker of orange had sent her into a panic. Then she'd set off on foot, running through the woods, slipping behind giant oaks and pines, the fear choking her like the clawing tendrils of a poisonous vine.

Creeping toward the east side of the lake, she stayed in the shadows, hunching low, searching for survivors. To hell with the proof. If she had a chance, she'd take Simon now.

Then she saw them. The Caldwell man wrapped his arms around Alanna Hayes and Simon.

Deep, painful breaths racked Phyllis's body as she began to sob, but she muffled her cries with her fists.

Thank God her baby was alive.

CAIN WAS SHAKING all over when he heard a siren wailing in the distance. He had to hide Alanna and Simon. If the police saw her, they might recognize her and ask questions. Questions he didn't know the answer to yet.

He froze, unable to believe he'd just decided to keep information from his own people. The police.

Alanna turned shell-shocked eyes up toward him and he didn't have a choice. He rubbed her arms. "We have to get you someplace safe while the firemen and police investigate."

"But where?"

"There's an empty cabin two doors down. Come on." Cain pulled her and Simon, rushing across the path through the woods toward the neighboring cabin.

An old man named Homer owned the place but rarely came up anymore; Cain kept an eye on it for him. Leaves crunched as the forest swallowed them. Alanna nearly tripped over a rotting tree stump, but he steadied her, well aware his own equilibrium was off-kilter from the smoke.

And from the fear that had nearly stolen his sanity when he'd see that man standing over her bed.

He kicked mud from his boots as he stepped onto the patio, then found the key in the old flowerpot. Darkness bathed the interior as they entered, but he switched on a lamp in the dingy kitchen. The place had been locked up for months and was cold and musty, but Alanna didn't seem to notice. In fact, she offered a fragile smile of thanks as he stroked her arm.

Admiration for her courage kicked in. "Wait here. I'll be back as soon as I can."

Alanna raised Simon to her shoulder and patted his back as Cain ran outside. Seconds later, Cain stood in front of his smoldering cabin, explaining to the firemen that he had woken to the smell of smoke.

A police car careened up the driveway and screeched to a halt. His partner, Neil Wakefield, jumped out and ran toward him. His captain, Bobby Flack, lumbered up the graveled driveway on his heels.

"What the hell happened?" Flack asked.

Wakefield's relieved gaze swept over him. "Are you all right, Caldwell?"

"Yeah." Cain rammed a sweaty smoke-scented hand through his hair. "All things considered."

"How'd it start?" Flack asked, eyes narrowing.

Cain watched the firemen douse the last of the flames, smoke spewing into the heavens, only the shell of his home still standing. "Someone broke in and set it."

Wakefield seemed shocked. "Arson?"

Cain nodded. Everything he'd owned had been inside. But none of it mattered. Except for the cross. His hand automatically went to the gold chain in his pocket, one of the reasons he'd had to go back inside. That and his gun and cell phone. He'd also managed to retrieve Polenta's gun.

Flack cocked his jaw sideways. "Do you know who set it?"

Cain shook his head. "No, but the man who broke in is lying in the ashes."

Wakefield winced. His captain chewed his cheek. "Someone have it in for you, or do you think it's related to Eric's death?"

"A lot of possibilities," Cain said, falling back on the fact that all cops made enemies and that his brother had a dozen as well. At least the excuse would buy him time.

Wakefield took charge. "We'll get an ID on the man, find out why he tried to kill you or if he's working for someone."

Cain's mind raced. If they found evidence of Alanna... "Thanks. I want to get to the bottom of this."

"We will, Cain."

Cain turned to his partner. Could he trust Neil to keep Alanna's identity a secret?

ALANNA SNUGGLED Simon to her, quieting his cries with a lullaby as she looked out the window.

"Fire."

"What did you say, sweetie?"

Simon's pudgy cheeks ballooned as he chomped out the words again. "Ma...ma. Fire."

A smile lifted Alanna's lips. At four and a half months, he was ahead of himself, a sure sign that his intelligence might be above normal. She stroked his baby-soft hair, her heart tugging painfully as his lips worked into a smile. "You are a strong little guy, you know that? I keep dragging you all over the place, but you bounce right back."

Despair threatened to overcome her. Even if she escaped these thugs, would their lives always be like this? Would they always be on the run? Never able to stay in one place for long or make a home?

Simon seemed oblivious to her turmoil. As if he trusted her to take care of things.

"I love you, Simon," she whispered. "I wish I could give you a normal family with a mama and a daddy and a house with a yard and a dog."

Or a cabin by the lake. Only now Cain's cabin was gone. He'd not only lost his brother but his home because she'd asked for his help.

Simon sucked his thumb until he fell asleep, his blind trust, intelligence and resiliency amazing her.

"Is that why they want you so badly? Do you have some kind of superintelligence?" A tree limb scraped the window and shadows hugged the spider-coated glass panes. Was someone outside?

Panic gripped her. At the graveyard there had been

two men. Had the other one been watching when they'd run from the burning house and followed her here?

"YOU THINK the intruder could have something to do with your brother's death?" Wakefield asked as the firemen rolled up the water hose. A team of investigators had shown up to examine the crime scene, taking photos and shuffling through the debris that had once been Cain's home.

He and Wakefield had already donned gloves and trudged over broken glass, charred furniture and smoldering wood to get to the body of the man who'd broken in. "I guess it's a possibility." A distinct one, but he didn't want to say too much.

"But if the guys after Palmer killed Eric to get at Palmer, why come after you? Unless they thought you're hiding the feds' witness?"

Cain glared at him. "I'm not hiding the witness. What happened with that John Doe burn victim?"

"Still no word." Wakefield eyed him carefully. "You're keeping something from me, partner. What is it?"

"Since when did you become psychic?" Cain muttered sarcastically.

"I'm not, but I've worked with you long enough to know you've got a hunch who did this." Wakefield gestured toward the smoldering ashes and waterlogged furniture on the ground. They both spotted the body of the man who'd broken in at the same time and jumped over a patch of smoking wood to get to him.

"This guy set the fire, but I don't know who he is yet."

The captain waved from the edge of where the front porch had been. "Found some matches and gasoline here. A pretty unsophisticated job."

Cain nodded and Wakefield leaned down to examine the charred body. An hour later, the scene had been swept for evidence, and photographs had been taken.

Wakefield scavenged through the remains of the bedroom, paused and knelt as he studied something on the ground. Cain's gut clenched when he saw the object. Neil arched a brow and turned to him with questions in his eyes. He'd found Simon's pacifier. It had somehow escaped the blaze.

"Since when do you have a kid?" Wakefield asked.

Cain winced. He might be able to explain a woman's things, but a baby's?

"Caldwell?" His captain interrupted, issuing orders as the crime team gathered samples and evidence bags and prepared to leave. "Let me know if you need anything."

Cain nodded and shook his hand. "Thanks."

Neil hung back, as if still waiting on an explanation. Cain had been partners with him for five years; if he couldn't trust him, there was no one he could trust.

"I'll ride back with them, you bring the squad car," Flack told Neil.

Neil nodded and waited until the others had driven

out of sight. "All right, buddy, tell me what's going on."

"You're not going to like it."

Neil's sun-bleached eyebrow rose a notch.

"I need you to keep this between the two of us."

The other brow shot up.

"For now, at least." Cain pulled his friend aside, then spilled the entire story, starting with how he'd met Alanna, his own skepticism over her story, and the events of the last few days.

"Are you crazy? Her name and picture are all over the news and the papers," Neil said through gritted teeth.

"Maybe." Cain shrugged. "But I do believe she's protecting this baby, and we know for sure now that someone will kill her to get him."

"You think the thug who set the fire came after the child?"

"Yes. He had his hands on Alanna when I busted into the room."

"Did Polenta hire the guy to come after her?"

"I don't think so. Alanna said he helped her escape with Simon. He sent her here to Eric."

Neil's mouth twisted into a grimace. "And you took her word for it?"

"No. But you told me freaky things were going down on Nighthawk Island. And Alanna...well, she's scared."

Neil studied him through slitted eyes. Cain shifted, his gaze taking in the remnants of his home, then flickering toward the woods and the cabin where he'd hidden Alanna.

"Geesh, you've fallen for this chick, haven't you?" Neil asked.

"She's not a chick, she's a woman who needs our protection." His voice rose an octave. "You don't understand, Neil, I think the baby is involved in some sort of research project. I couldn't find a birth certificate on him and I found files from the center that referred to him as Project Simon."

Neil pulled out a cigarette and lit it, his expression calm. "All right, say something strange is going down on Nighthawk Island. Say you believe this Hayes woman." He glanced around the lake, as if he suddenly realized she had been there but now was missing. "Where is she?"

Cain hesitated. "Someplace safe for now."

"You should report her, Cain. Don't be stupid like your brother."

Anger flared inside Cain. "Eric wasn't stupid. He was a brave man who tried to help women that the system failed." Even as he defended Eric, questions nagged at him.

He had never recognized those shades of gray existed until now. Had never told Eric how much he admired him for fighting for his cause. "Just help me keep Alanna's identity under wraps until I can get to the truth."

Neil opened his mouth to argue when the sound of a boat sputtering across the lake caught Cain's attention. Suddenly the hair on the back of his neck shot up. The man who'd broken in had been about the same size and height of one of the men who'd followed Alanna to the graveyard.

Where was the other one?

The fishing boat that had anchored in the cove all day…

Fear hit him as the realization sank in. Good God, had the men been watching them all day? If so, was the other man still lurking around?

Had he seen Cain take Alanna to the deserted cabin?

Chapter Twelve

A scraping sound outside the cabin sent an alarm up Alanna's spine. Then she thought she saw the doorknob turning. She flipped off the small lamp, pitching the room into darkness, and waited silently, nerves on alert. Had the other man from the graveyard followed her here?

If so, she had to hide.

Wincing as the old wooden floors squeaked, she slipped down the hallway, peering through the shadow-filled rooms. Two small bedrooms shared a tiny bathroom, both cluttered with dusty ancient furniture. A cobweb touched her hair as she inched inside the last bedroom, the scent of musty linens stifling as she turned the cold knob on the closet door. Her pulse clamoring, she slid inside, burying herself and Simon against the wall behind a knot of hanging clothes. Alanna prayed that if the man had followed her, he wouldn't find them.

"Listen, Neil, I've got to go."

"Go where?"

Cain felt for his weapon. "To check on Alanna and the baby. Two men shot at us the other day, and one of them died here tonight. I don't know where the other one is."

Neil stared at him long and hard. "Are you sure you know what you're doing?"

No. "Yes. Just don't tell anyone about her and the baby. Not until we find out the truth about what's happening." Cain's chest ached with worry. "I can't let Eric's death count for nothing."

"All right. But you could lose your badge over this."

Cain fisted his hands by his sides. Last week that thought would have kept him from crossing the line. But the memory of Alanna and Simon huddled in his arms, needing his protection as they'd run from the fire clinched his decision. He didn't have time to analyze his actions. "Keep me posted about Palmer?"

Neil nodded and Cain tore off into the woods at a dead run, grateful he'd grabbed his gun as he searched the forest for intruders. A dog barked somewhere in the distance and twigs snapped beneath his boots. Birds twittered and flapped in the trees above. The five-minute trek felt like hours, but he finally slowed, letting his gaze scan the area surrounding the cabin. The first thing he noticed was that darkness engulfed the dilapidated wooden structure. The light he'd turned on in the kitchen wasn't visible from the woods, but as he ran to the kitchen door, he realized it had been extinguished.

Had Alanna turned off the lights or had the man who'd followed them here?

His sweaty palms gripped the doorknob as he looked around the stoop for footprints or signs of an intruder. He saw nothing. All senses on alert, he slowly opened the door, craning his head to listen for voices.

An eerie silence greeted him, leaving him cold.

He crept through the cabin, down the hall, into the tiny bathroom, past one small bedroom, then to the end.

The man wasn't inside. But neither was Alanna.

Cain started back down the hall. Had Alanna gone outside? Had she run away? He searched the shadowy den once more, but the faint sound of a baby's gurgle brought his head around. She and Simon were still in the house somewhere. "Alanna? Where are you?"

Silence.

He crept back to the first bedroom and checked it again, then tiptoed to the second. "Alanna, where are you? It's me, Cain."

The door squeaked open. "Cain?"

She ran toward him, her heart in her eyes, and he opened his arms and embraced her. They clung together for several seconds. He breathed in her sweet scent, crushing the baby between them. Adrenaline quickly drained from him, leaving him weak-kneed. Exhaling a shaky sigh, he raked his hands over her hair, down her sides, then cupped her face in his hands and forced her to look at him. "You scared me to death."

His rough admission seemed to surprise her. It surprised him, as well.

In the past few days, she and Simon had come to

mean more to him than a case, and he knew it. But the reality of that realization scared the hell out of him.

"I was scared, too," she admitted in a hoarse whisper. "I thought I heard someone outside, then I remembered there were two men at the graveyard.

He nodded. "And only one in the house—"

"So I turned off the light and hid." Her shivering body convulsed against him. "I'm so glad you came back for us."

He rubbed a knuckle over her cheek. The need to hold her and protect her was overwhelming. "Did you think I wouldn't?"

Her thin shoulders lifted slightly. "I wouldn't blame you if you turned us in. My God, Cain, you lost your brother—" her voice broke "—and now your cabin, because of me."

Guilt darkened her blue-green eyes to an almost purplish hue. He remembered the pain in her voice when she'd mentioned her ex-husband, how he'd left her because she couldn't have a child, and he pulled her into the vee of his thighs. So close her legs brushed his.

"This is not your fault," he said, realizing he believed the words as he spoke them. He lowered his hand and stroked Simon's chubby hand, smiling when the little boy opened his eyes and peered at him so trustingly. "But we have to find out exactly who wants Simon and what they plan to do with him."

DAWN ROSE on the horizon by the time they'd both settled down. Exhaustion pulled at Alanna as she fed

Simon a bottle and rocked him back to sleep. Simon seemed slightly pale, adding to her worries. Cain stood guard at the window, searching the fading darkness for signs the other man had followed them.

With a featherlight kiss, she placed Simon on the extra bed in the first bedroom, then returned to the dingy kitchen. "Cain, I've been thinking."

His forehead creased into a frown.

"Maybe I should find the monastery that your brother used and let them help me go underground somewhere. It's not fair—"

"No."

His sharp tone took her aback. "But why not? I've already caused your brother's death."

"We're not certain about that."

She chewed her lip. "Well, we're fairly certain that you lost your cabin because of me. And you could have lost your life."

Cain's eyes darkened. "Is that why you want to leave? To protect me."

"I don't want anyone else hurt because of me." Her voice quivered. "I'm the one who ran away with Simon to protect him. You and your brother just got dragged into it."

A flash of something sexual sparked in Cain's eyes as he moved toward her. Tension rippled between them for one long heartbeat before he pressed a finger to her lips. "Maybe you did drag me into it, but I'm involved now, and I'm not running."

"But—"

"No buts." Hunger filled the air between them. "I want to see you and Simon safe. Not having to live on the run. You can't honestly tell me that's what you want."

Alanna shook her head slowly, the touch of his finger against her mouth so erotic she couldn't resist pressing her lips to the tip. The heated look that erupted on his face nearly took her breath away. Then the subtle tension was gone, and desperate, savage hunger appeared in its wake.

The harsh way he pulled her to him should have frightened her; instead the intenseness of his passion was titillating. His mouth captured hers, seeking, yearning, expressing his desire to claim her, and she succumbed to the pleasure, reveling in the play of his tongue along her mouth. Seconds later, his tongue teased her lips apart, torturing the inner recesses of her mouth, and his hands began a sensual trail along her spine.

Fingers teased and stroked her back, then slipped around to the underside of her breasts, causing her to swell against his touch. She threaded her fingers into his hair, hanging on his every movement as he lowered his mouth to nibble at the sensitive shell of her ear, then to the tender skin of her neck. He made her feel desired. Wanted. Loved.

Feelings she'd thought had died with her divorce.

His masculine scent enveloped her although the smokiness from the fire still lingered. The memory of their brush with death only fueled her hunger more, and she slid one foot up and down his calf, smiling as he growled into her ear. His hands circled her breasts, first cupping the small mounds, then teasing her nipples through the thin cotton sleep shirt she still wore. The muscles in his legs bunched against her thighs, his sex swelling and hardening, pushing toward her stomach, triggering a surge of moisture to pool inside her. Dropping her hands to cup his butt, she released a throaty moan, silently telling him she wanted more.

But the telephone jangled, breaking into their lovemaking with the sharpness of a siren. Cain hesitated, then slowly lifted his head and looked into her eyes. Passion glazed the dark irises along with regret.

"I'd better get that. Why don't you lie back down," he suggested softly. "You have to be exhausted."

She nodded. Quivering with longing and emptiness as he pulled away, she hugged her arms around her middle.

"We will finish this," he murmured in a hoarse whisper.

She couldn't reply, could only watch as he snapped his cell phone open. He stepped outside to answer the call, leaving her achy and alone.

DAMMIT. His old FBI buddy Luke had rotten timing. Cain hated to leave Alanna trembling from his touch, but hopefully he'd get some information that might help him save her and Simon. And find Eric's killer.

"Caldwell here."

"Hey, man, it's Luke."

"What did you find out about CIRP and Project Simon?"

"Not a lot. Polenta is not only a renowned geneticist but a humanitarian. Seems he had an infant son born with severe mental defects. The baby died shortly after birth. The incident inspired him to switch from internal medicine to pursue genetic disorders and genetic engineering.''

''Any specifics on his most recent work?''

''I talked to Denise Harley, the doctor who was kidnapped last year. She was working on a research project to increase cognitive growth at the fetal stage. When the company tried to sell the work out from under her, she destroyed the files. But she admitted it's possible someone copied the file before she could destroy the data. Or that they might have expounded on her work.''

''So, what are you saying?''

''There was some speculation about creating a superintelligent child.''

Simon? The baby appeared normal, although he was only four and a half months old.

''Their specific study isn't approved for human testing yet. All that controversy over cloning and stem cell work has slowed down approval while groups address ethical issues.''

''But someone could have experimented on the side. And since the human studies weren't legal yet, whoever had done them would want to keep things quiet.''

''Right. And they'd want to keep Simon nearby.''

''How about overseas? Would it be possible to sell the work to another country?''

''Sure. Some foreign governments don't have as stringent requirements as the U.S. Just like some countries have banned human cloning while others haven't actually taken a stand. Animal cloning is becoming more common, and the University of Georgia has one of the foremost cloning centers in the world.

"Now, tell me why you're so interested in all this." Determination hardened Luke's voice. "Do you have information on the attack on Polenta and his missing baby?"

Cain hated to lie to his friend, but he'd already told one too many people about Alanna. "I don't know yet," he hedged. "But if I find something, you'll be the first to know."

Cain hung up, troubled by what he'd learned. Proving his speculations would be difficult. Keeping Alanna and Simon safe in the meantime would be even more difficult.

His body hardened simply thinking about the beautiful woman lying inside. A few minutes ago, he'd been ready to take her. He'd momentarily forgotten the repercussions of a personal involvement. But he couldn't forget.

He had too much baggage to get attached to a woman, and a job that kept him at odds with normal life. She would want permanence, a man to stick around and be a father to Simon.

And he wasn't that man.

LATER THAT AFTERNOON, Alanna fed Simon a bottle, then settled him into the car seat so they could drive to town for supplies. All of Cain's clothes and toiletries had been lost in the fire, as well as hers, and Simon needed more formula and diapers. The poor baby had been unusually fussy all day, adding to the mounting tension between her and Cain. Worry pricked at Alanna, and she constantly checked Simon for a fever and signs of illness. Of course, he might simply be reacting to her anxiety. Babies were sensitive enough to do that and Simon seemed especially perceptive.

Cain had confiscated an old ski hat and overcoat for her from the cabin where they were staying and gave her tips on blending into the crowd and not drawing attention to herself.

Any evidence of his earlier hunger for her had disappeared. In its place, he wore a mask of calm detachment. She had no idea what had happened, but he'd resorted to giving her impersonal looks and keeping his distance. She missed the gentle touches and passion in his eyes, but reminded herself not to let his withdrawal bother her.

She would have to leave him soon, find a new identity. And when she did, she would never see Cain again. It would be foolish of her to fall in love with the man. She'd only end up hurt.

A small voice inside her head warned that it was too late, that she had already fallen for Cain.

"All right, stay close to me in the store and keep your head down." Having purposely driven to a neighboring town where he thought he wouldn't be recognized, Cain unfastened Simon's car-seat belt and lifted him out. Once again, his masculinity and size struck her as powerful, at odds with the gentle way he handled Simon. She tried to act nonchalant, as if the three of them were a normal family out for their Saturday shopping, not criminals on the run whose house had just erupted into flames the night before at the hands of a merciless killer.

The cold chilled her to the bone, adding to the icy tension between them as they rushed inside. They shopped for food, baby supplies and toiletries, then Cain grabbed two flashlights with batteries, a few inexpensive articles of clothing for him, mostly jeans and flannel shirts, then he added two packages of boxers and two packages of briefs. She tried desperately not to imagine him in the cotton underwear, but her imagination soared out of control. Then it was her turn, and she wished she was anywhere but beside him. They bought denim shirts, a sweatshirt and two pairs of jeans before she was forced to endure the lingerie section. Cain had no qualms about picking up a matching set of black silk panties and bra for her. She glared at his selection, then grabbed some cotton underwear and tossed them into the cart as well.

For a brief second, the hunger returned to his eyes as they passed a row of teddies, but it disappeared the minute they stepped up to the cashier's line. A stack of newspapers flanked the register, her own face plastered on the front page.

"Woman Kidnapper Wanted. Dr. Paul Polenta Wakes From Coma And Pleads For His Baby's Return."

Alanna's stomach pitched. Simon began fussing, drawing attention to them, and Cain took him from her, playing daddy to divert attention. The police were looking for a woman on the run with a baby—alone— not a family, he'd told her before they'd entered the store. Thankfully, her long blond hair in the photo and the hat changed her appearance enough to disguise her.

"Shh, it's all right," Cain said in a soothing tone, his words meant for her as much as Simon.

She unloaded the items onto the conveyor belt, grimacing when Cain picked up one of the papers and tossed it onto the pile. A security guard strode in and stopped to survey the store and Alanna nearly jumped out of her skin. But once again Cain calmed her by throwing his arm around her and pretending they were man and wife.

"Hey, darlin'," he drawled, then looked at the teenage store clerk, "me and the wife are going to have us a little second honeymoon."

The girl rolled disinterested green eyes layered in sparkly purple eyeshadow. Alanna nudged closer to Cain, grateful to have his strong arms holding her up as the security guard loped by.

CAIN HATED seeing the fear in Alanna's face and almost regretted taking her out in public, but they had to have supplies. Simon had started fussing again the minute they'd strapped him back in his car seat. Alanna's worry raised his own anxiety. Going to a doctor would be the curse of death for them, but it was a reality Alanna would have to face at some time in the future. A future that meant hiding out with a new identity, most likely. Far away from him.

Another reason for him to remain detached.

But if he exposed the truth about Simon and arrested the people after her, she wouldn't have to run. Was Alanna right—would Simon's chances for a normal life be destroyed if his birth circumstances were revealed?

Things certainly had been easier when he'd lived his life in black-and-white.

He maneuvered his car along the back roads, keeping one eye on the rearview mirror to confirm they didn't have a tail. Alanna's face blanched as she opened the newspaper. A photo of a brown-haired man lying in a hospital bed with dozens of tubes attached to his body and a white bandage around his head had been plastered below the headline, "Dr. Paul Polenta, Victim Of Brutal Attack When Deranged Woman Steals Baby."

Her horror-stricken gaze met his. "I swear this is not true. I never hurt Paul."

"I know." Cain laid a hand over hers to calm her, fighting the urge to drag her in his arms again. But her gaze had faltered when she'd seen Polenta's photo. What was her relationship with the man? Had they been more than friends?

When they arrived back at the lake cabin, they unloaded their purchases in strained silence and slipped into the dark interior. Cain remained on alert for anyone who might have followed them or sneaked into the cabin while they were gone. Hoping to calm her with some mindless television, he flipped on the set. But ten minutes later, her mood grew even worse when a special news report flashed her picture onto the screen.

"Ladies and gentlemen, we have a new turn in this sad story. Dr. Polenta, the man attacked in Savannah, Georgia, has finally come out of his coma. He asked to appear on camera in a plea for the return of his infant son.''

Cain moved toward the couch where Alanna sat, wide-eyed. The camera switched to the hospital where Polenta sat hunched over in a wheelchair. Obviously still in serious condition, he coughed, his pallor a sickly green, his eyes listless.

The reporter pushed a microphone toward him and Polenta, in a weak voice, his words slightly slurred, said, ''Please, Ms. Hayes—''

''Oh, no, Paul, what have they done to you?'' Alanna whispered.

''Please bring my son back...to me. He...'' Polenta's voice broke into a weak cough. ''He has a medical condition.'' His cough escalated so badly the reporter was forced to take over and read his statement.

''We've just learned from Dr. Polenta that his son has a special medical condition that is not readily visible. Blood tests show abnormalities that indicate he has a genetic liver disorder.'' The reporter paused, the camera zeroing in on Polenta's weakened form.

Polenta coughed, then cleared his throat. ''Please, Ms. Hayes, Simon needs a doctor. You have to bring him back to me.''

Chapter Thirteen

Alanna gripped the edge of the denim sofa, her head spinning. Was it true? Did Simon have a liver disorder? His pallor had been off earlier, and he'd certainly been cranky.

And poor Paul. He looked deathly ill himself. What had they done to him?

"It could be a trap," Cain said in a low voice.

"I know." Alanna's fingers dug into her palms as he sat down beside her on the sofa. "But what if it's true?"

Cain pulled her hands into his, warming them. "Don't panic. Just tell me what you know about Simon's medical history."

Alanna struggled to think about the early days when she'd first come to care for him. "He was born six weeks early. His lungs weren't fully developed so he had to have oxygen and he stayed in the ICU neonatal unit for several weeks. But I don't recall anything about a gene abnormality or his blood count being off. He was jaundiced but that's not uncommon."

"Who were the doctors in charge of Simon?"

"Dr. William Forrester was the OB-GYN who delivered him. Dr. Randall Ames and Stanley Peterson are heads of the fertility clinic. I met them when I went there for treatment." The bitter memories surfaced, but she quickly banished them. There was no time to dwell on her own problems and inadequacies. She couldn't let Simon down.

"This announcement about Simon having a medical problem could be a setup to lure you back to them."

Alanna clenched his hands. "I know, but what if it's not? Simon has been irritable lately and he looks peaked. All signs of illness."

"Don't babies sense stress from their caretakers?"

"Yes, but he still might be ill." Alanna's throat clogged with tears. "I don't think Paul would lie. He cares about Simon."

Cain studied her, his expression grim. "They might have drugged Polenta and forced him to make that plea."

"I can't take that chance, Cain. Simon has to see a doctor."

Silence reigned between them as they both contemplated the problems of finding a qualified physician with the expert training to care for Simon and one who'd keep their existence a secret.

Alanna stood and paced across the room, her nerves raw. "I have to call Paul and talk to him myself, Cain. Maybe he'll tell me whether or not they forced him to say that Simon is ill."

"If someone coerced him into saying those things, they'll probably be waiting for your call."

"That's a chance I have to take." She threw up her hands in frustration. "I couldn't bear it if Simon needed medical treatment and I did nothing."

"If the people there are forcing Polenta to make these statements, they probably have Polenta's phone tapped. At best, they'll try to trace the call so they can locate you."

"They already know I'm in Atlanta. They have to be the ones who sent those men after me."

He conceded her point, but he didn't look happy.

"I have to call Paul, Cain. I have to know if I should take Simon back to him."

Cain warned her to watch the time in case someone at the research center traced the call. "Paul looked so weak," Alanna said as she punched in the number. "I hope he can talk."

His eyes narrowed but she didn't have time to question his thoughts. The sight of Paul's photograph in the paper, and of him being wheeled to the microphone on the news broadcast had wrenched her heart.

"Coastal Island Research Hospital, how may I help you?"

"Dr. Polenta, please."

"Dr. Polenta is in serious condition, ma'am. He's not to be disturbed."

"This is important. Please put me through."

"Who's calling?"

Alanna nibbled on her lower lip. "Just tell him it's about his son."

The woman clucked a suspicious sound, but transferred the call to his room. Alanna glanced at Cain for support. Cain had claimed the ancient rocking chair and cradled Simon in his arms, smiling as the baby sucked on the bottle. At least Simon's appetite was intact; that had to be a good sign.

"Hello."

"Yes...Paul."

"Alanna?"

"Yes, it's me. God, are you all right?"

"I...I'm weak, are you okay?"

"Yes, I saw you on TV. I don't know what they did to you, but you have to tell me if Simon is really sick."

A bitter cough attacked him and Alanna held her breath waiting. "He...needs to be seen. Blood tests came back. Abnormal."

Alanna's legs gave way and she sank onto the sofa, hands trembling. "Tell me where to go. Is it an emergency? Can a regular doctor take care of him, Paul?"

"Have to bring him to me. Has to do with the project, the gene therapy."

Alanna's mind raced for a solution. "Are they holding you? Can you get out and meet me somewhere private?"

"I'll try. My office."

Cain tapped his watch and Alanna nodded. "We'll leave right away. But how will I get in touch with you?"

"Call my new cell phone. I'll sneak out of the hospital and find you." He recited the number.

Alanna hung up, her anxiety mounting as Simon began to fuss after he finished his bottle. "We have to go, Cain."

Cain nodded, his eyes wary. "Let me phone for backup."

"No." Alanna grabbed his arm. "I'll take Simon alone. You can't call the cops or the FBI."

Cain caught her hand in his, squeezing hard. "You're not going alone, Alanna. We're in this together now."

Relief mushroomed inside her even as she told herself it was wrong for her to accept his help. If the meeting was a setup, she didn't want another Caldwell man's death on her conscience. But she didn't want to die, either.

Then who would take care of Simon?

THE RIDE TO SAVANNAH took forever. Late-afternoon thunderstorms darkened the sky and slowed traffic to a crawl, afternoon rush hour adding to the torturous nerve-racking trek through the downtown Atlanta area. Winter vacationers heading south added to the mass of cars piling onto the expressway, several accidents up and down I-75 creating a backlog of impatient drivers.

Simon's intermittent crying mingled with the splatter of rain, increasing the tension in the car. As they drove down I-16 and neared Savannah, Cain pulled at the collar of his shirt, perspiration trickling down his neck in spite of the cool temperature outside.

"Shh, sweetie, don't cry." Alanna tried to quiet Simon with a pacifier and toys, to no avail.

"Do you think he's sick?" she asked, an edge to her voice.

Cain gave the baby a once-over. His cheeks had lost their pale color, but he was screaming, which probably accounted for the pink flush. "Does he feel warm?"

Alanna pressed a hand to his forehead. They had taken his temperature before they'd left and it had been normal. "No."

"Maybe he's teething."

Hope flitted across her face for a brief second. She slid a finger inside his mouth, feeling his gums. "Maybe. But I can't feel any teeth coming through."

"Could be too early."

Alanna nodded, obviously latching on to his reasoning. "Maybe we can stop at a convenience store, so I can buy some numbing gel to rub on his gums. Oh, and a teething toy."

Cain nodded and flicked the radio station to a soft jazz station, hoping it might calm them all. Simon's cries slowly faded as he drifted asleep.

"Go ahead and get some rest, too," he said.

Alanna lay her head back and sighed. "Aren't you tired, Cain? I know you didn't sleep much last night."

He patted her hand, his body tingling at the feel of her soft skin beneath his fingers. "I'm used to long hours. A cop's work."

A few miles down the road, she relented and exhaustion claimed her.

Cain remained tense, on alert, head spinning with questions. The past hour had seemed endless. Alanna had moved beside him, her head leaning on his shoulder. Something about the gesture seemed very intimate, stirring emotions and thoughts he had no business feeling. His own anxiety over Simon's health didn't help either, adding to the bigger worry that they were walking into a trap.

But the realization that he cared about both Simon and Alanna kept him from pulling her into his arms. Once they discovered the truth about Simon and he'd found a way to insure Alanna and Simon had a life together without scientists on their tails, he would have to say goodbye to them. And move on to another case. He'd have to prove Eric's innocence in the Banks murder.

The heaviness in his chest built like a slow throbbing pain.

He pulled into a convenience store for gas. Alanna and Simon both stirred. "Why don't you feed him while I run in and get some of that numbing gel."

"Thanks, Cain."

He filled the gas tank, then went inside to pay and picked up the medicine, but the afternoon edition of the paper drew his eye. The front page featured an article about genetic engineering and recent scientific breakthroughs. Apparently Polenta's plea for his son had spurred a piece on his work and other related topics. Cain paid for the items and hurried to the car, tossing the paper on the seat. Alanna flinched at the sight of the front-page article, then picked it up and read silently while Simon sucked down formula. "This certainly puts Paul in a positive light."

Cain twisted his mouth in thought, knowing she was right. The more positive Paul looked, the less sympathetic Alanna would appear in the public's eye.

Alanna flipped open the paper. "There are more articles on the research center here and the cancer vaccines they've been working on. The experiments with stem cells are the most controversial, but they're working in reproductive biology to transform stem cells into organs chemically."

"That process would eliminate the unethical element of using human embryos, right?"

"Right, but it's probably years away."

Cain considered the articles about Arnold Hughes and the problems at the center in the past year. Even with the negative publicity the center had garnered, one or two bad apples in a barrel of thousands of geniuses couldn't negate the cutting-edge work conducted at CIRP.

Still, the media attention would only add to the cloud of doubt hovering over Alanna should she be discovered now. If Polenta had warned Alanna not to go to the press, why had he or the people behind Project Simon done so? Weren't they afraid Alanna would come forward and tell them her suspicions?

Exactly the reason they had leaked the story first, he realized. Putting her on the defensive definitely gave them the advantage. After all, whoever instigated Project Simon at CIRP could tamper with files and records to disprove her claims.

If that happened, how the hell would he ever prove Alanna's story was true?

Details of the article about Hughes's supposed death flashed into his mind. Hughes had disappeared at the same time Denise Harley's work had supposedly been destroyed. Could Hughes have survived and accessed her work? Could he be the mastermind behind Project Simon?

SAVANNAH GREETED THEM with its magnificent historical squares, carriage rides and giant azaleas flanking the streets, taking Alanna back to the day she'd first moved to the quaint Southern city to take care of Simon. A time when she'd just experienced her husband's rejection and learned she couldn't bear children of her own, a time that had been the lowest point in her life. But the rich Southern landmark had welcomed her into its loving arms, embracing her with the cultural hospitality famous in the South. Then she had met Simon and the cloak of darkness that had surrounded her had melted into a ray of light that spelled hope. Simon had given her a reason to live, a reason to believe that she could find happiness one day, a child to love and fill the empty void in her life. Now he lay snuggled in his car seat, sleeping, oblivious to the fact that danger dogged him like a demon. That she might lose him any moment.

The scents of salt water and fish assaulted her as they drove out of the downtown area along the coast, then crossed the bridge to Catcall Island, the first of the islands in the Coastal Island Research Park. A sliver of a moon flitted off darkened sandy beaches, only an occasional jogger braving the earnest wind rolling off the ocean. The screech of the wind outside reminded her of the legend of the island, and the reason for its name—Catcall. Locals claimed when the wind blew the tall sea oats, it sounded like the low mewling sounds of a cat calling out for help. The sound mirrored her own silent cries.

How could she fight a conspiracy by the scientists involved in Project Simon when she didn't know which doctors were involved and when she had no proof to back up her story? The articles in the newspaper hailing the center's work made her look even more guilty.

"You're awfully quiet," Cain said.

"I'm just worried about Simon."

Cain's hand enveloped hers, stirring titillating sensations inside her as well as troublesome ones. He had stuck beside her through this entire ordeal and she had finally begun to trust him.

But she couldn't allow herself to give him her heart. If she found out Simon was healthy, she had to obtain a new identity and leave him behind.

Cain cleared his throat. "Where's Polenta's office?"

Alanna pointed out directions. Cain had checked over his shoulder a thousand times but hadn't noticed anyone following them. They wound through the research park, then through the archway created by towering ancient oaks. Hopefully, they could sneak in and meet Paul, and she'd learn the truth about Simon's health without anyone catching them.

CAIN SWORE SILENTLY at the security he spotted around the research park, his instincts on alert for a setup. He'd watched for a tail the entire way to Savannah, even more so when they'd crossed onto the island, but saw nothing, which aroused his suspicions even more. Instincts warned him that someone had orchestrated this meeting to lure them back, yet he didn't know how to circumvent the trouble; they had to know if Simon needed medical treatment. He'd considered calling for backup, but then he would have to expose Alanna. Even though he'd told Wakefield about Alanna, she had no idea Cain had taken the man into his confidence. Plus, bringing along cops would only draw more attention to them and force the issue of going public with Project Simon.

"You need to phone Polenta."

Alanna nodded and punched in Paul's number while he studied the shadows darkening the main hospital building.

"Paul, it's Alanna. We're here." She listened quietly for a moment, her hand trembling as she disconnected the line.

"He's going to meet us behind Building A. His office is inside. He can help us through security."

"How did he sound?"

"Weak."

"Could you tell if he'd been drugged?"

Alanna shrugged. "I'm not sure. He sounded… worried."

Pausing to cup her face in his hands, he met her gaze, interjecting as much confidence in his voice as he could. "It's going to be all right."

She nodded, jutting up her chin in a show of courage that didn't quite meet her eyes. Cain felt inside his jacket for his gun, praying he wouldn't need it. Seconds later, he led the way, coaching Alanna to stay behind him with Simon so he could scope out the area. Wind howled from the distant marshland, the sounds of night frogs and crickets adding to the grating whine of the salty breeze.

Weeds bent at their feet as they circled to the back of the building. Cain remained alert for night watchmen, grateful when the only visible one headed in the opposite direction, toward the tip of the island.

"Shh, Simon, honey," Alanna whispered over the sound of rustling leaves.

Cain hesitated, ushering her beneath the awning of the building. The creak of a wheelchair broke into the night. Alanna clutched his arm, digging fingers into his jacket as they waited.

"Paul?"

He tried to hold her back, but the minute she saw the shadow of the man rolling toward her, his efforts obviously labored, his breathing ragged in the pungent air between them, she stepped from behind him.

The man's eyes were listless, his voice a mere croak when he finally spoke, "Simon." Polenta tried to lift a thin-boned hand but failed.

"Paul, you have to tell me if Simon is really sick—"

"...showed me bloodwork—"

The man never finished the sentence. Suddenly all hell broke loose. A gunshot pierced the air, two hulking security guards jumped Cain from the rear, two more grabbed Alanna. She screamed, crying out in anguish, as they tore Simon from her arms.

Chapter Fourteen

Cain fought off the attackers and reached for his gun, but another man fired, and a bullet slammed into Cain's chest. His body flew backward, and blood gushed from his lower shoulder. He pressed a hand to his chest, shooting off a round from his gun. But he missed the shooter when the man ducked behind the building. Alanna fought and kicked, trying to hang on to Simon, but one of the men jerked the baby from her hands, then pinned her arms behind her. A third man pushed a gun toward Polenta's temple and wheeled him away. The man holding Simon turned to follow him, but Alanna screamed out and clawed at the man. He turned and slammed the butt of his gun against Alanna's head and sent her flying to the ground.

Cain struggled to get up, to save her and rescue Simon, but his head spun and he swayed. Taking quick advantage, the beefy guard slammed his fist into Cain's injured shoulder. White-hot pain seared through Cain, and he saw stars. Another blow caught him in the gut, the next one connected with his nose.

The squeal of tires on pavement punctuated the air, as if someone had just driven up and screeched to a halt.

He threw his hand up to ward off another blow, but the attacker punched his face again. He heard the crunch of bone just before blackness engulfed him.

ALANNA HAD NO IDEA how long she'd been unconscious, but slowly, as the dim light from an outside bulb heightened the pain behind her eyes, reality returned. The stark agony of realizing they had taken Simon knifed through her.

Cain.

Dear God, she tried to sit up but a wave of nausea wreaked havoc with her equilibrium, and she struggled for composure. Then she saw Cain lying in a pool of blood. So much blood, gushing from a chest wound. The dark red blood had soaked his shirt all the way to his stomach.

Tears pooled in her eyes as she struggled to crawl to him.

Please don't let him be dead.

Inch by inch she dragged her aching body across the dirt, her pulse clamoring at the sight of a pair of headlights shimmering from the parking lot. Someone was watching them, their beady eyes trained on her. Who was in the car? Someone coming back to finish the job?

Panic seized her, but she scrambled over the rocks, the sharp points tearing at her hands, ripping the skin raw. She spit out dirt and fought a sob at the sight of more blood gushing down Cain's chest. He was so still. So pale. Where had he been hit?

She checked Cain's pulse, grateful to find one, although it was weak and thready and his breathing was shallow.

Her gaze cut across the property. Where had they taken Simon?

She wanted to run after her baby, to search the facility until she found him and took him back in her arms.

But she couldn't leave Cain here to die.

He'd been hurt trying to save her and Simon. And Eric was already dead....

She peeled back his jacket and checked the injury. The bullet had pierced his left shoulder, slightly above his heart. She prayed it hadn't gone into his lung. Knowing she had to stop the bleeding and get him to a hospital, she jerked off her sweater, then the T-shirt below, then firmly pressed the shirt onto his wound while she pulled the sweater back on to cover herself.

"Cain, can you hear me?"

Applying pressure to the bleeding, she searched the shadows for more attackers. "Cain, please wake up. We have to get out of here."

A low groan erupted from his throat, so she shook him gently again. "Please, Cain. Come on, I don't think I can lift you by myself." And dammit, she couldn't call the cops.

His eyes finally fluttered open, and seemed to focus on her face. Wind rustled the leaves around her and she spun her head around to see if someone was coming, but saw only darkness.

"They have Simon," she said in a strangled whisper. "But you're bleeding pretty badly. We have to get you to a hospital."

He shook his head, but Alanna slid an arm beneath his good shoulder and tried to pull him up. "Come on, I'm not arguing with you. Losing your brother was bad enough. I'd never forgive myself if you died because of me, too."

The grunt that followed echoed with pain and stubbornness, but together they finally stood and she half dragged, half pulled him to his Jeep.

Stumbling against the side of the car under Cain's weight, she opened the Jeep's door and heaved Cain inside. He fell into the passenger side with a moan and lay his head back against the seat, while she ran to the other side, jumped into the driver's seat and started the engine. Her own head throbbed from the blow she'd sustained, but she ignored the pain, knowing it didn't compare to the ache in her heart from having Simon ripped from her arms.

Cain groaned and passed out again and she hit the gas. She'd drive him to the hospital, then she'd come back for Simon.

PHYLLIS DROVE AWAY from the research center, worry gnawing at her. She almost had everything she needed to claim Simon. She'd thought it would be easier to take him away from Alanna than the doctors at the research center. But when she'd lost track of them after the fire, she'd nearly panicked. Then she'd seen Polenta's plea on TV and she'd known Alanna would return to CIRP. She'd driven here and waited. And waited.

But now Alanna had lost the baby.

Hadn't the little fool known she was walking into a trap? She'd thought the cop would have better sense. Of course, he was probably one of those macho guys who thought he was invincible.

Well, he hadn't been and they'd let the doctors get her son.

What should she do now?

She had to get that file. Prove Simon belonged to her.

She drove to a pay phone and checked the home address for the OB-GYN who'd delivered her baby. Five minutes later, she turned onto the small Isle of Hope and wove past the different street signs until she located the sign for the doctor's street. Three houses down, she parked along the street and strode toward Dr. Forrester's small cottage, relieved at the sight of lights glowing inside. No doubt, he would be surprised to see her.

Determination filling her, she knocked on the door, tapping a high heel impatiently when he didn't immediately answer. Her agitation mounted. She pounded the wooden door, noting the fading chipped paint and weathered hardware, frowning at the fishy scent of the ocean drifting in with the late-night breeze. One hand patted the outside of her leather purse, folding over the security of her .22 resting inside.

The door creaked open, and the elderly white-haired doctor appeared, rubbing the bridge of his nose with pinched fingers. "Yes, what…" Recognition dawned in his eyes. "Ms. French, what can I do for you?"

"I want all the files about Simon's birth, including his birth certificate. It's time everyone learned that he's my baby."

"But you had a miscarriage. Simon—"

Phyllis slid the gun from her purse. "I know what you told me. I also know that you and the other doctors at the fertility clinic lied to me and that nurse you hired to take care of Simon."

ALANNA PACED the waiting room of Savannah Hospital's surgical wing, her mind replaying the terrifying moments just before Cain was shot, when Simon had been taken from her. Aching and empty now, she curled her arms around her middle, grieving for the void his absence caused.

Her only consolation was that if Simon did have special medical needs, the team of doctors responsible for Project Simon, whatever the hell *project* meant, would take care of him.

But would she ever see the baby again? Would they ship him off to some remote lab and isolate him from the world? Would he ever have a normal life?

"Miss, you're the woman who brought that police officer in?"

"Yes." She glanced up at the doctor, praying he didn't recognize her. When she'd dragged Cain in with a gunshot wound, he'd given her a suspicious look, as had a couple of the nurses, but Cain had managed to stay awake long enough to identify himself as a detective and to offer a cover for her.

Legalities necessitated the doctor report the incident, so Cain had begged him to call his partner in Atlanta instead of the locals, and not to inform the press of his injury. The doctor had reluctantly agreed. Cain had claimed Alanna was a witness under protective custody, and that leaking the story to the press would jeopardize her life and blow a major undercover investigation. It wasn't really a lie, but would they believe the story if someone recognized her from the photo that had been plastered all over the news?

"He's out of surgery now and resting, if you'd like to see him."

A huge sigh of relief escaped her, which felt far more personal than she wanted to admit. "How is he?"

"A little uncomfortable and weak from blood loss, but he'll be fine. The bullet went into his shoulder but thankfully missed his lungs and heart. I'd say he was pretty lucky."

She followed the doctor into the recovery area, a small space surrounded by sterile sheets and filled with the strong scent of antiseptic and other hospital smells that had once been a part of her daily routine. Though she was a nurse and the steady beep of the IV and the other tubes and paraphernalia didn't shock her system as it often did regular patients, her stomach rolled at the sight of Cain's ashen face. His dark hair looked mussed and stuck to his head where he'd sweated, rough beard stubble darkened his wide jaw, and his lips looked parched and dry.

She moved toward him slowly, knowing the doctor was watching, although she heard him slip away, obviously to offer her some privacy. For a moment she simply stared at Cain, memorizing his features, the strong set to his stubborn jaw, the slant of a nose that had been broken before and was swollen now, the sooty-black lashes that curled down on normally bronzed skin that had lost its color. He was devastatingly handsome and the strongest, most honorable man she'd ever known. He had put his own life and career in jeopardy to protect her and Simon while grief stricken over the loss of his brother.

He did it all to find his brother's killer, a little voice in her head whispered.

Only she remembered the heated kiss and hunger in his eyes and wondered…

No sense fantasizing over things that could never be. If she found Simon again, she would disappear and never see him again. She had to in order to protect him.

"Cain? Can you hear me?" She gently lifted his limp hand in hers, smiling as his rough, callused palm enveloped hers.

A low moan escaped him as if he was fighting to come out of the anesthesia.

"Thank God you didn't die." The tears she'd been fighting rose to the surface and spilled over. His other hand found its way into her hair and he opened his eyes, the regret and sorrow so strong that it broke her heart. "I'm so sorry, Alanna."

Then, in spite of his injury, he pulled her down to his chest and held her while she cried.

IGNORING THE THROBBING in his arm, Cain stroked the base of Alanna's neck to comfort her, knowing her emotional release had been long coming. He was grateful she had held herself together long enough to get him to the emergency room. But she had lost the baby she loved and her heart was breaking.

He couldn't believe he had failed her and the little boy. Just like he had failed to protect Eric.

Guilt pressed against raw emotions, fear for the baby boy he had come to care about twisting like a knife in an already sore gut. Dammit, what was he going to do now?

He sure as hell couldn't stay here in the hospital.

"Your head?" he murmured, his throat so dry it felt like sandpaper. "Are you all right?"

She nodded against his chest and her soft hair tickled his chin, the sweet scent of her shampoo arousing his senses, obliterating thought of the pain in his shoulder. "We'll find Simon," he heard himself promise, although he had no idea how. He needed help, and a phone to call his partner and his buddy from the FBI.

A sob escaped her, but she slowly lifted her face, her tearstained big blue eyes luminous with sorrow. "I'm sorry I got you involved in this, Cain. S-so sorry you got hurt."

Ah, God. He raised a shaky hand and threaded it through her hair. "Shh, I'm a cop, remember? I've been shot before." He gritted his teeth, fighting the ache in his shoulder as he tried to move. "Will be again. Goes with the territory."

Her raised eyebrow said that it didn't matter, because this time he'd been shot because of her.

"I'm going to find Simon and protect him, so stop blaming yourself," he said in a gruff voice. "Now, see if you can find my cell phone."

She sniffed and wiped her tears, her courage once again earning his admiration. "You can't use it in the recovery room."

"Then help me get out of here."

"Cain—"

He gripped her chin in his hand. "I don't intend to lie around in this bed when we have to find Simon."

Her look of concern pulled at emotions deep inside him, awakening them from a long-dormant sleep. How long had it been since a woman had actually cared about him? Even his mother had put herself before her sons.

"You forget that I'm a nurse, Cain. I can't allow you to leave when it could be dangerous for you. You've lost a lot of blood."

"I'll do it with or without your help."

She sighed and pressed a hand to his cheek, the gesture so tender that again his heart tripped over in his chest. "Every second counts, Alanna. I lost Eric. I don't want Simon to be lost, too." He brushed a tendril of hair from her forehead. "Eric would want me to help Simon." And you, he added silently. He probably would have fallen in love with you, too.

Too? He jerked in shock at his own thought, nearly ripping the IV from his arm.

She soothed him with tender fingers, running them across his chest, and he silently cursed for enjoying the sensation so much that he almost begged her not to stop.

"Let me talk to the doctor first, then I'll see what I can do about getting you to a phone."

He nodded and watched her leave the recovery room, a piece of his heart going with her.

ALANNA ASKED the nurse to page Cain's doctor, then stepped into the privacy of the waiting room, trying to avoid eye contact with as many of the staff as possible in case someone recognized her. The portable TV blared from the corner, the news reiterating the story about Polenta's missing baby, flashing her old photo. Then a special series featuring several scientific research projects aired, one centering around a child who'd surgically received a heart valve from an animal. The poor little girl had borne the brunt of brutal jokes by classmates and the tabloids, reinforcing Alanna's reasons for wanting to keep the research around Simon confidential.

Cain's comment about every second counting ticked through her mind like a time bomb—did he think the doctors might be taking Simon someplace far away? If they would kill her to get him, what else would they do to cover up his existence?

The thought sent a shudder through her.

Footsteps clicked on the faded linoleum of the hospital corridor. She looked up expecting to see the doctor. Instead, an auburn-haired woman she guessed to be in her mid-thirties stepped inside the small room, buttoning a taupe suit jacket around a pudgy midriff. Dark green eyes slid over Alanna, the thin-lipped smile mirroring the animosity in the woman's expression. Alanna moved to the rear of the room and flipped off the TV set, figuring the woman had come to visit an ill friend or relative. But she strode straight toward Alanna, throwing back her shoulders as if to intimidate her. "Miss Hayes, we need to talk."

Panic zinged through Alanna. She tried to scoot around the woman, but a hand much stronger than it looked reached out to dig pink fingernails into Alanna's arm.

Alanna's gaze swung to the woman's as she silently struggled for a handle on the situation. She certainly didn't want to bring attention to herself.

"What do you want?" Alanna asked.

"To talk to you about Dr. Polenta."

The blood froze in her veins. "What?"

"Let's sit down. I don't want anyone to hear us and I know you don't."

Weak with worry and shock that the woman knew her identity, Alanna sank into the nearest vinyl chair, the sharp edge digging into the backs of her knees. "Who are you?"

"My name is Phyllis French. Tell me everything you know about Simon."

Chapter Fifteen

"What?"

"You heard me correctly," the woman said. "I know who you are and that you took Simon from the Coastal Island Research Park."

Alanna angled her head away from the doorway as a nurse walked by. "Who exactly are you? And what do you know about Simon?"

Phyllis French's eyes turned cold. "I'm a reporter for the *Savannah Times*. I've been investigating the research center ever since that story broke on Tom Wells last year."

Alanna faintly remembered the bizarre study involving memory transplants and cringed.

"I also know that the doctors at the fertility clinic have been conducting follow-up work to that research Dr. Harley did last year, and I'm sure Simon is a product of it."

"What makes you think that?"

"I posed as a woman needing fertility treatments and went to the clinic for testing." Phyllis French perked up like a peacock spreading her feathers. "I'm quite the ingenious investigative reporter, you know."

"No, I don't know." Alanna stood, ready to bolt. "And if I believed a baby was involved in something as horrendous as a research project, I certainly wouldn't talk to the press."

"Listen, Ms. Hayes, what you don't seem to understand is that I'm on your side here. I don't like what they're doing with Simon and I want to print the truth."

"The truth might turn his life into a nightmare."

Her icy hand touched Alanna's arm. "And I could turn yours into one if I expose you. Now tell me what you know about Project Simon."

The thinly veiled threat sent Alanna's pulse skyrocketing.

"Look, Ms. French." She rubbed sweating palms together. "I don't know the details surrounding Simon's birth. I only want to give him a normal life. And printing a story about him will do exactly the opposite."

"Even if that story exonerates you?"

"I don't care about myself, just Simon."

"What about Simon's real mother. Do you care about her, Ms. Hayes?"

"His birth mother abandoned him—"

"Is that what they told you?"

Alanna could only stare at her and nod. What did this woman know?

Phyllis French pressed a shaky hand to her chest.

"Well, that's not true. His mother loved him and wanted him very much."

"You know who his mother is?"

"Yes, and I also know the name of his father, but I can't reveal that information until I have proof. Now tell me, does the baby really need special medical treatment like Dr. Polenta suggested on that news report?"

"I...I don't know." Alanna saw Cain's doctor heading toward her in the hall, extracted herself from the demanding woman's hold and darted away. The sooner she and Cain left the hospital, the better. Phyllis French might expose her to the police, then they'd lock her up and she'd never see Simon again.

But she hesitated as she reached the doorway, wondering if she'd been too hasty in her exit—if the reporter knew the name of Simon's birth mother, did that mean she was alive? Did this woman know her whereabouts? Did Simon's mother want him back?

And what about his father? Did the man who'd donated his sperm and helped create Simon want him as well?

CAIN'S SHOULDER and arm ached, fiery pinpoints of pain stabbing him as the anesthesia wore off. But he'd waved off the nurse's offer of pain medication. He needed all his faculties in order to think straight. Endless seconds ticked by to the drip of the IV while he waited on Alanna's return. The cold, white sheets draped in the recovery area added to the claustrophobic effect of the hospital.

He hated being helpless.

Knowing little Simon needed his help fueled his energy, spiking a temper he tried hard to control. One that threatened to erupt any second. He had grabbed the IV needle to rip it loose when Alanna pushed back the curtain and slipped inside.

She laid his jeans and jacket on the end of the bed. "They had to cut off your shirt."

He retrieved his pants, almost panicking when he reached inside his pocket and felt nothing. Had the cross fallen out when he'd been shot? Willing himself to remain calm, he checked the other pocket. The moment his hand closed around the gold cross, his chest expanded with relief. A tender smile softened the lines around her mouth when she recognized the object in his hand, but faded before it made it to her eyes.

Cain pressed the necklace to his chest. "Get me out of here."

"Tomorrow," she said, her voice unsteady. "They're moving you to a room right now."

Cain cursed. "I need to get out of here now, Alanna."

She laid a trembling hand over Cain's. "It's nearly midnight, Cain. There's nothing we can do until morning. Besides, the doctor absolutely refused to release you, and from a medical point of view, I agree."

He glared at her, willing her to change her mind. But he could tell by the firm set of her fragile jaw she wouldn't budge. Tenacious, gutsy, courageous—all the qualities he admired in her were the ones that had landed her in this situation. Ones that would have to help her through in case...no, he wouldn't allow himself to believe that they wouldn't find Simon.

That she would never hold the baby she loved in her arms again.

That was not going to be a reality, not like Eric's death.

The overhead light accentuated the bruises beneath her eyes and her own exhaustion. Something else had happened while she'd left him. "Did the doctor say something to upset you? He didn't recognize you, did he?"

She shook her head, while a team of orderlies entered the room. They both quieted while they rolled Cain to a hospital room. Once the men had him settled in for the night, he motioned for her to join him by his bedside. She stood hesitantly, the fear and agony in her eyes a thousand times more painful than his gunshot wound.

"Alanna, I know this is difficult—"

"A reporter approached me in the waiting room," she said in a rush. "She asked about Simon."

His heart stopped beating in his chest. "What else did she say?"

"Simon's mother may still be out there looking for him. And so might his father."

"Do you have any idea who his parents might be?"

Alanna shook her head. She swayed on her feet, and he pulled her toward him. "Come here and lie down. You need some rest. You probably have a concussion yourself."

"I'm fine."

"You're anything but fine," he growled. "Now climb up here."

She followed his instructions while he dragged himself to the edge of the narrow hospital bed. "We'll find Simon," he said in her ear. Careful of his injury, she rolled on her side and laid a hand on his stomach. "I know you want to raise him yourself, Alanna."

She nodded against him. "I do. I love him more than anything." With a weary sigh, she lifted her head and looked into his eyes, the sadness there nearly breaking his heart. "But if Simon has a mother or father who want him, who really love him and can offer him a normal life, I'll have to give him up."

Cain pulled her into his arms. He prayed it didn't come to that.

But he also knew she might be right.

PAUL POLENTA LEANED into the wheelchair as Stanley Peterson, one of the heads of the fertility clinic, shoved him into the small hospital room on Nighthawk Island where they had been holding him prisoner. He lifted a weak hand, trying desperately to fight the effects of the drugs they'd pumped into his system, and tugged on Peterson's sleeve. "Tell me the baby's all right."

Peterson glared down at him over his bifocals.

"Simon is fine. We're running tests on him right now to make certain."

He sighed in relief. At least the baby hadn't been hurt in that horrible ordeal back at his office, the one he had helped create because he'd had a gun pressed to his head and he'd been too much of a coward to die. Memories of his family back home in Italy floated through his drug-induced haze. He would probably never see them again. Maybe it was better. He didn't want them to know what he'd done.

"How about Alanna?"

Peterson parked the wheelchair in the corner and folded lab-coated arms across the chest that housed his inflated ego. "That was your mistake, Polenta, falling for the woman."

Paul ran a shaky hand through stiff, sweat-soaked hair. "Just tell me she's still alive."

Peterson shrugged. "Put her out of her mind and focus on your work. Right now that's the only reason you're still breathing. When you agree to keep quiet about Project Simon, you can return to the lab." With a flick of his wrist, Peterson produced a syringe, grabbed Paul's weakened arm and jabbed him with the needle.

Paul gripped the edge of the wheelchair, wishing he had the energy to fight. But his limbs were leaden, his head spinning as the slow crawl of drugs seeped through his system. A heavyset nurse lumbered in and assisted him to the hospital bed, but he heard voices in the open doorway.

The other scientist, Ames.

"Did they get the woman yet?" Peterson asked.

"No, someone drove up in the parking lot and they had to let her go." A pause. Paul strained to keep his eyes open, his mind alert, but his eyes drifted shut.

"They have to find her and that cop."

"We've been staking out the nursing home where her grandmother is. Odds are she'll show up there to check on her while she's here in Savannah."

"What about Simon's father? Do you think it's time we brought him in on things? He's anxious to return to CIRP."

"Not yet. But soon. Very very soon. Meanwhile we have to protect his interests."

Paul gritted his teeth, biting his tongue when he tried to call out and tell them to stop. God, no. The last thing they needed was Simon's father to resurface…

ALANNA SLOWLY STIRRED, the warmth beneath her cheek so heavenly she didn't want to move. She'd been dreaming she lived in a beautiful lake house with a white picket fence. And in her dream, she'd shared the house with Simon and Cain.

But reality returned with a bleep of the IV and the realization that Cain had been shot, that he didn't love her, and that she no longer had Simon.

She might have lost him for good.

Mind-numbing pain seared her.

Worse, even if she and Cain found Simon, the baby might have parents out there searching for him, wanting to claim him as their own.

She opened her eyes, the early-morning sunlight filtering through the hospital blinds a reminder that another day had come, though this one held emptiness and the promise of more sorrow instead of the joy of a baby in her arms.

Pushing the hair from her face, she lifted her gaze to check Cain and found him watching her. His dark gaze skimmed over her, filled with troubled emotions and a sensuality that vibrated through her.

On the heels of awareness rode guilt. How could she even think about sex or the strength of his embrace when her baby was missing?

Because she needed comfort…

He ran his thumb gingerly along her shoulder blade, then pressed a gentle kiss into her hair, his tenderness like a soothing balm to her shattered nerves.

"You ready to get me out of here?"

She smiled in spite of the grief consuming her. "If the doctor says it's okay."

"To hell with the doctor.

"Cain, you've been shot—"

"And I'll live. Where's my phone?"

She slowly sat up, then grabbed his jacket from the chair beside the bed and collected his phone.

"Why don't you see if you can round me up a shirt while I check in. I need to see if my partner has found anything on Eric's killer."

Alanna nodded and stood, stretching sore muscles as she tried to ignore the loss she felt when Cain released her. They might have an attraction brewing between them, but she couldn't kid herself. They both needed comfort now, but when this ordeal ended, when they found Simon or his parents took him, Cain would return to work as a cop in Atlanta and she would have to move on alone.

CAIN'S HANDS clenched in frustration as he watched Alanna slip out the door, the devastation he'd seen in her eyes a mere shadow of the anguish he knew she had experienced over losing Simon. Remembering she couldn't have children of her own added to the equation. But the fact that she loved this baby so unconditionally that she'd risk her life for his welfare negated any selfish motivation he'd suspected she might have had.

Would it be possible to put Simon back in her arms? Especially if his birth parents came forward to claim him?

Cursing beneath his breath, he punched in his partner's number, kicking at the sheets as he reached for his jeans. His arm was sore and still connected to the IV, so he couldn't manage the phone and dress at the same time.

"Wakefield here."

"It's me."

"Why the hell didn't you answer your phone? I've been trying to get in touch with you all night. Are you okay?"

"I'm fine. What's going on? Did you learn something new about Eric's killer?"

"No. But guys at the Twenty-Third figured out who killed Charlene Banks's husband."

"Who?" Not Eric, please not his brother.

"Seems he had a girlfriend on the side. She didn't tolerate being a punching bag like Charlene had."

His breath whooshed out. "Do Wade and Pirkle have any leads on Eric's murder?"

"Fingerprints from Eric's place included prints from that missing witness. So it looks like Eric had been covering for him."

"Palmer's probably in hiding now."

"We're still waiting on DNA for that John Doe burn victim at Grady."

Hopefully the John Doe was the witness.

"Now, tell me what the hell happened, Caldwell."

Cain swore, then relayed the events of the past twenty-four hours, beginning with the trap Polenta had set and ending with his injury.

"Dammit, Cain, you should have called me in as backup."

"Alanna would run like crazy if she knew I'd confided in you."

"Alanna?"

"Yes, Alanna," he snapped. A long pause followed, filled with questions that Cain refused to answer.

"You really think this broad's on the level?"

"I didn't at first, but I do now. She loves the baby and wanted him to have a normal life. I just wish I knew what had gone down at the center."

"I can tell you this, bud, the cops are going to be

combing Savannah looking for her. Have you seen the news this morning?"

"Hell no, what now?"

"The OB-GYN who delivered Polenta's baby was murdered last night. And guess who the prime suspect is?"

He muttered a violent oath. He didn't have to guess. He knew without his partner telling him.

Alanna.

ALANNA VENTURED as far as the elevator near the nurse's station when she caught a heavyset nurse with curly red hair peering at her over her computer. Another nurse, this one pushing sixty with wiry gray hair, whispered and reached for the phone.

The hair on the back of Alanna's neck prickled. Not wanting to draw suspicion to herself, she turned away, hoping they hadn't recognized her. Then she edged herself against the door, punched the elevator button and strained to hear their conversation.

"I think it is her," the redhead whispered.

"She brought that cop in with a gunshot wound."

"You think he's protecting her?"

"If he is, we have to turn him in, too. She's not only a kidnapper, but now she shot and killed that OB-GYN—"

Alanna's blood constricted, her head spinning. She had to escape.

Adrenaline pumping through her, she slipped into the shadow of the doorway, then turned and jogged back down the hall toward Cain's room. Panic seizing her, she shoved open the door.

"Cain, we have to get out of here now."

Cain was already sitting on the edge of the bed with his shoes on, tugging his jeans over his hips. His look of alarm only added to her anxiety.

"What happened?"

"One of the nurses recognized me."

"Damn." Cain jerked at the IV, but Alanna dashed over and disconnected it.

"Cain—" her voice broke "—they think I killed the OB-GYN who delivered Simon."

Chapter Sixteen

Cain grimaced. Being a suspect didn't necessarily bother him, but knowing his picture might soon be plastered all over the TV like Alanna's would definitely slow them down. He needed help, not only from his partner, but from the FBI. He'd phone Luke as soon as they found a safe place to hide.

Alanna slid an arm beneath his shoulder. As much as he hated to have to accept her assistance, he leaned against her while they hurried down the corridor. At the end of the hallway, they met an orderly who gave him an odd look, but he simply smiled. "Just stretching the legs."

The man nodded and ambled on, pushing a cart of juice and magazines.

Footsteps indicated a team of doctors approaching. He and Alanna ducked into an alcove containing soda and snack machines, then picked up the pace until they reached the elevator. Just as it dinged open and they climbed inside, more footsteps pattered behind them.

"There they go," one of the nurses called.

Cain hit the down button and held his breath while the elevator descended.

"If they stop us, I'll turn myself in," Alanna admitted. "I won't let you take the blame for my actions."

He squeezed her arm and shook his head. "We'll find a way out of this mess, Alanna. I promise you." The door opened and they stepped out, dodging a security guard talking on a walkie-talkie. Ducking into the crowded emergency room, they tried to blend with the crowd as they wove their way outside. Dewy grass made their trek slippery, the hum of thick morning traffic a reminder that life for some people was normal.

A few harrowing seconds later, they ran toward Cain's car. The stitches in his shoulder pulled, but he ignored them.

Twenty minutes later, Cain picked the lock on an abandoned beach cottage on Skidaway Island outside Savannah, his conscience only slightly nagging at him. He'd considered a hotel but that would be the first place the police would look.

"I can't believe we're doing this," Alanna said. "We could be arrested for breaking and entering."

A wry chuckle escaped him. "Honey, a B and E charge is the least of our worries."

Alanna helped him inside, closing the curtains while Cain checked the rear. When he finally walked back to the tiny den with its threadbare furniture and wicker rug, she turned and clutched her head in her hands, looking as if she might faint any second from pure misery.

THE ROOM FELT as if it were closing in on Alanna. She had always been a good person, an honest citizen. She had never cheated on a test in school or hurt anyone intentionally.

But now she had caused the death of one man and the police wanted her for kidnapping and murder. The trembling started deep inside, so deep she felt as if her insides might explode. The agony of knowing Simon might be lost to her forever was too much to bear in the face of the morning sunlight.

"All I wanted to do was to protect Simon," she whispered in a thready voice. "I even left my grandmother behind to save him."

Cain's gaze locked with hers, his understanding look surprising her. "I know. And I'm sure he's all right." He moved toward her, but she couldn't accept his comfort, not when she'd caused him so much grief already.

"I should check on Gram while I'm here."

"It's too dangerous to visit her," Cain warned.

Alanna hugged her arms around herself. "Maybe I could at least call and see if she's all right."

He frowned. "Get a shower. I'll see if I can find us something to eat. Then we'll talk about calling."

"I'm not hungry."

"But you need to keep up your energy. We have a long fight ahead of us, Alanna." His voice grew low. "You can't give up now."

"What if the owner comes back here, Cain?"

"This place has been deserted for the winter. It was boarded up, remember?"

She nodded, although tears welled in her eyes.

Cain brushed a knuckle over her cheek. "I'll get the heat going. Go get that shower."

Alanna nodded and thanked him, then found the dingy shower.

But as she stepped beneath the warm spray of water, defeat settled over her. An emptiness threatened to consume her. She had done everything in her power to keep Simon and protect him.

But she had failed. And now Simon might be lost to her forever.

WHILE ALANNA SHOWERED, Cain searched the cupboard and found a box of pancake mix that seemed fresh along with syrup, and decided to make them breakfast. But first he had to clean himself up and call Luke.

He used the extra bathroom and washed up as best he could with his bandaged shoulder, wishing he had a razor to shave. Although a beard might help disguise his face if he needed it.

Using his cell phone, he punched in Luke's number, not wanting to phone the FBI directly in case someone had discovered that he and Luke had been in contact.

"Luke, this is Cain."

"God, am I glad you called. Where are you?"

"It's better I don't say."

"What's going on, Caldwell? First, you ask me to check into the medical research at the Coastal Island Research Park the same day a kidnapping at CIRP occurs, then last night there's a murder, and now you won't divulge your whereabouts."

"Trust me, if I get in trouble over this, I don't want you going down with me."

A long silence ensued. "You know something about that OB-GYN's murder, don't you?"

"I don't know who killed the doctor. But Alanna Hayes didn't do it." Cain grunted. "You'll be the first to know if I figure out who did."

"All right, as long as you're certain you know what you're doing."

Cain glanced toward the back bedroom, his body thrumming with desire at the sound of the shower, at the mere thought of Alanna's naked body covered in soapy bubbles.

What was he doing? Lusting after a woman who might have caused his brother's death? Harboring a fugitive and diving headfirst through murky gray waters?

"Cain?"

"I do. Have you learned anything new about CIRP?"

Luke cleared his throat. "Nothing concrete, but word is that Arnold Hughes is actually alive and going to resurface."

Cain ran a hand down the peeling wallpaper. "You have someone on the inside looking for him?"

"Not yet, but we will." He exhaled. "Trouble is, we think he's had plastic surgery, so no one will recognize his face."

"Keep me posted."

"You do the same."

"Okay, but one more thing. See what you can find out on a woman named Phyllis French. She claims to be a reporter for the *Savannah Times*.'' Luke agreed, then Cain hung up, but a muffled sound from the shower jerked his mind back to Alanna. He shoved the phone into his pocket and moved toward the noise, disturbed by the sound. Alanna was crying.

Her violent sobs tore at him, resurrecting the grief that had consumed him since he had lost Eric.

One day soon Alanna would walk out of his life. Then what would he have left?

Rational thoughts fled and he pushed open the bathroom door, halting when he saw her back pressed against the steamy stall, her hands covering her face. Unable to stop himself, he grabbed a towel from the shelf above the toilet, opened the door and wrapped her in it. Surprised when she didn't protest, he patted her dry, his body thrumming with arousal at the sight of her slender frame glistening with water droplets. Her skin shimmered like gold, the iridescent softness of her skin beckoning his touch. His pulse clamored as the dim light of the bathroom flickered across pert rosy nipples, and glowed in a honeyed line down her flat belly to her sex below. His throat went dry.

But he didn't want to take advantage of her pain, so he enveloped her in a dry towel and hugged her to him.

''Cain, no, I've caused you too much trouble.''

''Shh, let me hold you.'' Emotions zinged through him when she turned those big blue-green eyes toward him. Hunger, need, loneliness echoed in the depths, a primitive call to his own empty soul.

An iron double bed draped in a simple white chenille bedspread filled the small bedroom that connected to the bath. Her gaze fell to his bandaged shoulder, to the dark hair on his bare chest, to the waistband of his jeans. An unspoken current of need, strong and potent, rippled between them. He'd forgotten he was half-naked himself, and was stunned when she traced a finger gently around the edge of the bandage. "Are you in pain?"

God, yes. But not from the gunshot wound. "No. A little sore, that's all."

"I'm so sorry I involved you in all this, Cain."

"Stop it, Alanna. You didn't start this, the people at CIRP did." He rubbed his hands up and down her bare arms, itching to strip that towel and touch her skin, to put some color and light back into her face and eyes, to make her forget all her troubles, at least for a little while.

But he couldn't do that without promising her more than a one-night stand, and he couldn't promise her more than tonight. Hell, he couldn't even promise her that he would be able to put Simon back in her arms, much less a happy-ever-after.

He turned to leave her to dress, to give her the privacy she deserved, to save himself from making a big mistake. But just as he turned, she caught his hand and brought it to her lips, then brushed the softest kiss across his fingers.

The urgency of her silent request slammed into him. He could no more walk away from her now than he could walk away from finding his brother's killer. Growling a low moan filled with pent-up savage hunger, he captured her mouth with his and took her in his arms.

ALL ALANNA KNEW was that she wanted Cain with a desperation that took her breath away. She threaded her fingers into his hair, drawing his mouth harder, firmer onto hers until his tongue made a luscious foray inside her hungry mouth and his sex hardened and surged against her belly. Then he tore the towel off and she stood like a virgin, shivering beneath the scrutiny of his passion-glazed eyes. The pain of losing Simon and the fear of almost losing Cain blended into a need so achingly deep that control completely slipped through her clutches.

He slid his hands down her shoulders, teasing nerve endings that sang from his touch, then slowly cupped her breasts in his hands. She almost protested, remembered how her ex-husband had found her lacking, but this was different. This was about offering comfort. Feeling alive again and taking away each other's pain for just a little while.

A smile curved his mouth as he pinched her nipples with his fingers and liquid heat pooled in her belly. Moaning, she traced a finger down his uninjured shoulder, then trailed her hands down to his waist. He quickly took off his belt and tossed it to the floor. His jeans went next, the play of muscles in his thick thighs wickedly delightful. She had never reveled in a man's body before, but the minute he unveiled his belly and then his sex, arousal rippled through her.

Hands that had held a gun the day before and protected her now slid across skin hot and fluid beneath his loving touch. Then his mouth and hands were everywhere, suckling, teasing, torturing her in every sensitive spot from the nape of her neck to the inside of her thighs to the tips of her toes. Alanna had never been loved so thoroughly.

Flooded by a rush of erotic sensations, she gently pushed him back on the bed and returned the favor, first flicking her tongue along his mouth, then dragging it down his neck and chest to his taut nipple where she paused to suckle him as he had her. He bucked beneath her, driving her wild as his sex jutted toward her heat, straining for entry. But she fought off the sweet release instead and lowered her head, tasting him as he'd tasted her, driving him wild with a wanton frenzy of hungry strokes until he called her name. He dragged her off him and pushed her onto her back. Bracing himself with his uninjured arm, he growled her name and gazed into her eyes, the raw primal need there mirroring her own. With a lick of his tongue down her breasts, he eased her legs apart and plunged inside her.

Alanna clawed his back, digging into his corded muscles as he rode her into oblivion, their sweat-soaked bodies moving together until they both exploded in ecstasy.

WHITE-HOT SENSATIONS spiraled through Cain, the room spinning with the intense heat still coursing through him. Knowing he was probably crushing Alanna, he lifted himself on his uninjured arm and forced himself to look into her eyes. The passion still shimmering in her gaze brought his arousal to life again.

"Don't move," she whispered, wrapping her arms around him.

"I'm crushing you." He gently eased off her but rolled her into his arms, dragging her close. He was sweating, but she didn't seem to mind. Instead, she traced a titillating finger through the hair on his chest, raking downward toward his belly. His sex throbbed, thick and full.

He told himself he should pull away. Get up and put some distance between them. But his emotions were too damn raw and close to the surface to leave Alanna just yet.

Somehow she had filled the emptiness in his soul with her courage and warmth, and he couldn't face returning to that hollow loneliness again. He cradled her head against his chest, tangling his legs with hers, and let himself enjoy the erotic feel of her breasts against him. Trying not to analyze the moment or their lovemaking too much, he whispered kisses into her hair and murmured nonsensical nothings into her ear until her raspy breathing slowly faded into sleep. Then and only then, did he allow himself to relax enough to join her.

CAIN BOLTED AWAKE at the sound of the phone ringing. He glanced at Alanna's sleeping form cuddled into the curve of his body and hated to move. But early-afternoon sunlight spilled into the room. He scrubbed his face over his hand, unable to believe they'd slept so long. Yet the sweet remnants of exhaustion from their lovemaking still simmered through him.

The phone.

Easing his arm from beneath her head, he slid his

legs over the side and pushed himself up, then dug in
the pocket of his jeans until he found it. He hurried
to the den.

"Caldwell here."

"Cain, it's Neil."

Something must have happened. "What's up, man?
Do you have some news?"

"Actually, I do." Neil hesitated, an odd note to his
voice that Cain couldn't pinpoint. Excitement maybe.
"You aren't going to believe this, Cain."

"What?"

"It's about that witness in the feds case."

"You found him?"

"We're not a hundred percent, but the John Doe
burn victim at Grady finally came out of his coma."

"It was the witness?"

"No."

He shot a worried look at the bedroom, his gut
pinching when Alanna strode to the door, wrapped in
the sheet, her hair mussed, eyelids heavy with sleep,
her cheeks pink from the rough stubble of his un-
shaven jaw. "Look, Neil, I'm not into games this
morning—"

"It's afternoon, and get this." His partner's voice
sounded odd. "The man in the hospital claims he's
your brother."

Chapter Seventeen

Alanna paused in the doorway, chastising herself for feeling so lonely when she'd woken up to an empty bed. She had been sleeping alone forever, it seemed, and she would be sleeping alone a lot more in the future. She knew better than to allow herself to get emotionally attached to Cain. Still, their lovemaking had been so intense and wonderful that the wall she'd built around her heart since her divorce had cracked, letting in a surge of feelings and wants that could only lead to heartache.

Cain's face suddenly paled, and he held the phone to his ear in a death grip. They couldn't face more bad news, not today.

"I'll be right there." Cain ended the call and his gaze flew to her, an odd expression tightening his mouth.

"What is it, Cain? Is there news about Simon?"

His mouth tightened even more. "I'm afraid not."

"Then who was on the phone?"

"My partner. There was a John Doe in the burn unit at Grady Hospital. The police thought he might be a witness to a crime they were hunting for, but the man woke up this morning…'' His voice trailed off, riddled with emotions.

''What is it, Cain?'' She crossed the room to him, pulled his hand in hers and rubbed the callused skin. Earlier those fingers had stroked her tenderly, igniting a fiery passion that still burned deep in her belly. Now they clung to her as if asking for silent understanding in return.

His gaze met hers. ''I don't know whether to believe it or not, but the man claimed he's my brother.''

She squeezed his hand. ''Oh, my God, is it possible Eric survived? I thought you said his car exploded.''

''It did. I watched it burn myself.'' His eyes narrowed. ''But somehow he must have gotten out and stumbled away. The man who died in the car must have been the witness the feds have been searching for.''

The ramifications of what Cain had said sank in. ''Then your brother is alive. Cain, that's wonderful.''

He embraced her, his body shuddering with the onslaught of emotions. She trembled in his arms. When he pulled back, a look of elation shone in his eyes, along with fear that he might get his hopes up for nothing. ''I have to go see for myself. He's been burned though,'' he said, his voice turning gruff.

''It won't be easy.'' Alanna rubbed a hand up and down his muscled arm. ''But at least he's alive, Cain. That's all that matters now.''

He left her arms to rummage through the duffel bag holding his clothes, then yanked on a denim shirt, wincing when his shoulder must have protested.

Alanna grabbed the sleeve and helped him slip it on, then fastened the buttons for him, her gaze flickering down to his unbuttoned jeans. His hot breath bathed her face, his masculine scent almost intoxicating. An awkward look passed between them that held regret, yet the simmering sexual spark sprang to life again, more intense than before.

She opened her mouth to speak but let the moment pass instead, refusing to spoil his happiness with an awkward conversation about their future. Or lack of one.

He cleared his throat, notching his belt. "I hate to leave but I have to drive back to Atlanta and see Eric."

"I'll get dressed—"

"No, Alanna, you need to stay here."

"What?"

He cupped her arms in his hands. "Right now the police are looking everywhere for you, not only for kidnapping but murder. You need to stay out of sight."

Panic seized Alanna as she glanced around the dusty, sparsely furnished cottage. "But I'll go crazy here just waiting. And what about you? You just had a bullet removed yesterday, Cain. Are you sure you're up to driving five hours?"

"I'm fine. But you have to be strong and hide out, for a little while longer, until the publicity dies down." He brushed a knuckle across her cheek. "I don't want to see you in jail for a crime you didn't commit, and every cop in the state has probably memorized your face."

"But you can be my alibi. You know I didn't kill that doctor."

"Yes, and when the time comes, I'll testify to that, but I want to get to the bottom of this Project Simon before I turn it over to the force." His voice pleaded with her to understand. "Besides, I can get in and out of the hospital faster to see Eric if I'm alone."

Alanna bit down on her lower lip, wavering. He was right. But the thought of him leaving only reminded her that she would be alone soon, for good. And possibly without Simon....

How would she go on?

He paused in the doorway, then retrieved the gun he'd taken from her earlier. "Do you know how to use this?"

She bit her lip. "Yes."

"Good. It's just for protection, Alanna." He brushed a kiss across her temple. "Don't shoot me when I return, okay?"

She forced a smile. "I won't." But as he hurried out the door, she locked it behind him, then paced the small confines of the cottage, the musty odor and drab walls closing around her.

She would go nuts today waiting on him, knowing Simon was out there needing her. She almost ran after Cain, but his warning resonated like a gong in her head.

She might go crazy here but it was better than being locked in a jail cell.

She put the gun on the table near her, then picked up the stuffed puppy Simon had grown attached to, memories of holding Simon in her arms bombarding her. He had called her Mama.

Was he sleeping without the stuffed animal? Was he all right? Or was he frightened?

Who would hold him and comfort him now when he cried?

CAIN WAS HALFWAY to Atlanta before he realized he'd forgotten his cell phone. He didn't want to turn back though, so he forged ahead, deciding he'd call Alanna after he arrived and saw Eric.

If the man was Eric.

He still couldn't be certain until he saw him with his own eyes. Only he'd supposedly been burned so badly that recognition might be difficult. His chest ached at the grim thought, his shoulder throbbing, but he parked the car and hurried inside the hospital. He'd simply be grateful if Eric was alive.

They would get him help, plastic surgery, whatever he needed.

Several minutes later after he'd stopped at two different nurses' stations, he found his partner waiting for him at the entrance to the burn unit.

"Have you seen him?" Cain asked, trying to catch his breath.

"No. The doctors are being very cautious with visitors. I spoke with them about you, though, and they've agreed for you to visit. But only for a few minutes."

"Did you get the fingerprint results?"

"We're working on that now, but his fingers were

burned pretty badly, so we may not get a hundred percent match.''

Cain stepped forward but Neil caught his arm.

''Listen, Cain, you need to be prepared...''

Cain's jaw snapped tight, but he nodded, forcing from his mind thoughts of the pain his brother had endured. He'd stay by his side and help him through every minute of recovery.

After a quick stop at the nurses' station inside ICU and a minute with the doctor in charge, Cain eased into the intensive care room, bracing himself for the sight of the tubes and machines and bandages the doctor had described.

Still his throat went raw.

The man lay so still he looked like death. Bandages covered most of his face and arms and chest, and his eyes were barely visible behind the layers of white gauze. Fisting his hands by his side, Cain strode toward him, his shoulder twinging.

He took one step, then another, until he was so close to the bed, he could reach out and touch him. But he didn't. He stared, tried to discern the man's features beneath the bandages, tried to study his height, body size, every clue available to identify him.

''Eric?''

The oxygen tubes attached to his nose twitched with his labored breathing. The man's eyes flickered open briefly, then closed, then he slowly opened them again. Pupils glazed from pain and pain medication sharpened his dark eyes to black but they were brown. Eric's eyes were brown.

''Can you hear me?''

The smallest tilt of his head indicated a yes.

"Are you Eric Caldwell?"

Eyes squinted and blinked, then slipped back into focus. "Eric?"

Another tiny movement of his head up and down, and Cain released the breath he'd been holding.

"God, man, I...I thought you were dead." His voice broke. He reached inside his pocket and gathered the gold cross in his fingers, then held it up to the light. "I found this outside your car."

Recognition dawned, a flicker of light erupting to replace the darkness in the man's eyes, then his fingers flexed from the edge of the bandage as if he were reaching for Cain.

For the cross.

"Mama," Eric murmured in a hoarse croak.

Emotions choked Cain as he laid the gold chain in Eric's fingers and watched him curl it into the bandaged palm of his hand. At that moment, he knew without a doubt that his brother had returned to him, injured but alive.

THE MINUTES AND HOURS DRAGGED by so slowly Alanna thought she would scream. Twice she almost left the small cottage to take a walk on the narrow strip of beach that backed up to the small island lot but reminded herself that Cain was right. The last thing she needed to do was be recognized or arrested; she'd barely escaped the close call at the hospital.

Was the man in the hospital really Eric? Had he survived the awful bomb and lived?

Prayer after prayer rattled through her head that

Cain would find him alive. That the brothers would be reunited.

And that one day she would hold Simon in her arms again as well.

She tiptoed to the window and peeked through the thin line dividing the two halves of the faded curtains, watching seagulls swoop along the rocky shore, searching for food. Nestled in the cove, rocks jutted out to form a jetty and waves crashed against their jagged surface, then receded to the infinite blue depths beyond. With winter at its peak, the only visitors in sight were the night crawlers or occasional sea turtle. The deserted stretch of beach overgrown with sea oats and broken shells stood virtually isolated, the perfect place for peace and quiet.

Yet there was nothing peaceful about how she felt. She had never been so lonely in her life.

Aching from missing Simon and Cain, she studied the seagulls' movements, her agitation growing as the sun dipped low into the sky, creating lines of orange and pink and yellow across the horizon. She wanted to walk that beach with Simon, collect seashells and search for crabs, dig for sand dollars on the sandbar where the tide rolled out.

A lone fisherman walked the distant beach near the pier, then stopped and propped his fishing pole against the primitive wooden dock. For a moment she froze, remembering that Cain had said the thugs who'd attacked them in his cabin had probably been spying on them from fishing boats on the lake that day. The phone trilled, startling her and she spied the man turn from the dock and walk her way. Though he was a good hundred yards down, she wondered if he could hear the phone. Should she answer it or not? What if it was someone for Cain?

Or maybe it was Cain calling to tell her about Eric or with news about Simon?

Or maybe he was calling to tell her the other thug was on her tail, that he had rented a fishing boat...

Panicking, she picked up his cell phone and answered the call.

"Caldwell?"

She cleared her throat and grunted a deep reply, waiting to see if the man identified himself.

"Listen, it's Luke."

Luke? Cain's friend from the FBI?

"Things have heated up around here concerning that investigation on Arnold Hughes. I know you're hiding the Hayes woman, but it's time you brought her in."

Shock and betrayal shot through Alanna and she punched the end button, then tossed the phone to the floor as if it had just stung her. Seconds later, the phone rang again.

The FBI agent calling back?

But what if it was Paul or one of the doctors with news about Simon? She'd left Cain's number on his voice mail in case he needed to talk to her.

She had to know if Simon was okay.

She took the call, her knees buckling when she heard Paul's voice.

"Alanna, listen, I can't talk, they may be following me."

"Where are you?"

"I got away. Can you meet me?"

"Yes. Where?"

"You pick the place. Somewhere they won't look for us."

"At my grandmother's nursing home. I want to say goodbye to her."

He started to say something but static cut in, destroying the connection. She hung up, remembering Cain had the car, wondering if she should call him. But she had his cell phone, and his friend's voice reverberated in her head. *Maybe you should bring the Hayes woman in.*

No, she couldn't let him know where she was going. She'd walk somewhere and find a taxi. Then if she and Paul found Simon, he could help her get away.

"SO, WAS THE GUY who died in the explosion the witness the feds need?"

Eric nodded, grief adding to the pain in his eyes.

"I know this is hard for you, man, and I'm sorry."

"I was going to bring Palmer back to trial," Eric mumbled brokenly. "He wanted to testify."

Cain nodded. "Do you remember anything about that day?"

"We argued…didn't kill Banks." Eric's voice was low and hoarse. "Helped his wife, but not a killer."

"I know. The cops discovered Banks had a woman on the side. She decided to make him suffer the way he'd made her suffer. Only she took it a step further and killed him." Cain dropped his head forward. "You don't know how much I regretted our fight that day, Eric. The last few days when I thought I'd lost you, all I could think about was how badly I felt that we fought. How I wished I could take it back.''

A tiny wrinkle creaked the bandage on Eric's forehead and Cain realized he was frowning.

''Not your fault,'' Eric mumbled. ''Stubborn.'' His gaze slid over Cain. ''What the hell happened to you?''

Cain had almost forgotten his own injury. He filled him in on the details. ''Sorry, man,'' Eric said. ''Didn't mean to get you involved.''

Cain chuckled. ''Don't sweat it. Things have changed in the past few days. I've changed.''

Another frown from his brother.

Cain told him about Alanna and Simon and the research clinic.

''Told her to come.''

''I know. I've been trying to find out what's going on.'' Cain placed a hand on his brother's, not wanting to add to his pain. ''I see the grays now, bro. Everything's not always black-and-white.''

''You're helping the woman and baby then?''

Cain nodded again. ''She's in hiding right now. In fact, I need to go back to see if I can find Simon.'' His throat clogged with emotion. ''But I don't want to leave you.''

Eric gestured toward the bandages. ''They're taking care of me here. Go on, do what you need to do to protect them.''

Cain touched his brother's hand, moisture filling his eyes. ''I'll be back, Eric.''

His brother nodded, his eyes already closing from fatigue.

Cain swallowed back a gambit of emotions and hurried to his car. He would take care of Alanna and Simon, then come back and take care of his little brother.

And he'd never second-guess him again.

CAIN'S ANXIETY GREW the closer he got to Savannah. Twice, he'd stopped and called his cell phone, only Alanna hadn't answered. Not that he'd expected her to. She was playing it smart not picking up his cell in case someone else had found her or traced her to his phone.

Alanna and Simon are not just a case. You care about them.

Ignoring the voice whispering in his head became impossible as he turned onto the street leading to the island cottages where he'd tucked her away earlier. He slowly checked each of the driveways, watching for a tail and any curious neighbors that might grow suspicious before he parked. The small clapboard cottage sat in darkness, spiking his nerves to a fever pitch. Maybe she was asleep. She might have gotten spooked and decided to keep the lights off so as not to alert neighbors, although the two cottages next door appeared to be uninhabited.

The hair on his neck stood on end as his boots clattered on the cobblestone steps leading to the side entrance where he'd broken in earlier. Hedging his movements, he slipped inside, pausing to listen. Eerie darkness and quiet had settled over the beach cottage, the musty odors assaulting him.

Seconds later, his heart came to a halt when he realized the cottage was empty.

Chapter Eighteen

Cain had lied to her. He'd promised not to involve the FBI, yet he had betrayed her and done just that.

Had he planned to turn her in all along?

Was that the reason he hadn't wanted her to accompany him to see his brother, so he could alert the feds to her whereabouts and have them pick her up?

The bitter taste of distrust lingered in her mouth as she exited the taxi she'd taken from the corner near the beach cottage. She searched the thin stream of people on the sidewalks and street near the nursing home where her grandmother resided, pulling the old ski hat and coat she'd borrowed around her, ducking her head to avoid eye contact as she wove her way up to the front door.

Flanked by concrete pots of fake geraniums and pansies, the staff had tried to add color and life to the gray stucco building where so many elderly people lived. Her grandmother...had she missed seeing Alanna the past two weeks? Did she even realize she hadn't been in to visit?

Her heart heavy with Cain's betrayal and worry

over Simon and her only living relative, she slipped almost soundlessly down the corridor to her grandmother's private room. Would Paul be inside?

Halfway down the hall, she spotted a nurse exiting one of the rooms and ducked into the supply closet, emerging seconds later wearing a crisp nurse's aide's uniform. Carts holding juice and books clinked along with the sounds of nurses' laughter and the whine of hospital machinery in the background. It was almost midnight; her grandmother would most likely be asleep.

It didn't matter. Alanna had come to say goodbye. And to meet Paul.

Fingers curled into a knot, she sneaked into her grandmother's room, pausing to drink in the sight of her frail form lying in the hospital bed, brittle gray hair fanned across the pillow, the peace of sleep softening her aging features. Before illness had claimed her, her grandmother had loved her unconditionally. What would she think about Alanna's actions the past few days? How would she react if she knew her granddaughter was wanted on felony charges, that she'd been accused of kidnapping and murder?

As she moved closer, she wondered if her grandmother had had one of her good days today or if she'd suffered from those terrible memory losses that stole her mind. Maybe it was a blessing she wasn't fully aware of the news events of the world now and Alanna's place in them.

A wave of sadness washed over her as she pulled the stiff vinyl chair up beside the hospital bed. Surprisingly, her grandmother opened her eyes and smiled, almost as if she'd been waiting.

"You did come today," she said a low voice tinged with sleep. "Oh, and you've been to work?" She indicated the uniform with a gnarled finger.

Alanna tucked her grandmother's hand in her own, letting the warmth of the elderly woman's fingers seep through her own cold ones. "I love you, Gram."

Her grandmother smiled, her gray eyes twinkling. "It's late though, child. You must be exhausted."

Alanna smiled. She was tired, tired of running and being alone. "I'm fine, Gram. How was your day today?"

Her grandmother giggled like a schoolgirl. "Good, Evelyn gave me a manicure. She painted my toenails shocking-pink, too."

Alanna unfolded her grandmother's hand and admired the bold pink shade on her nails, remembering a time when Gram had painted Alanna's nails for her. She wanted to stay and take care of her.

But if she found Simon, she would be on the run again.

They chatted for several more minutes about mundane things. Alanna laughed at her grandmother's story about the older man in 7B beating her at bingo, but soon fatigue coaxed her grandmother back into sleep.

"I love you, Gram." *I may not be back for a while, but remember that I love you.* Alanna placed a kiss on her grandmother's hand, then gently covered her up with the blanket. Taking one last look at her beloved face, she turned and walked away.

''Take care, sweetheart,'' her grandmother whispered.

''I will.'' Alanna squeezed her eyes to ward off the tears as she closed the door behind her. She had to find Simon, and if she did, *when* she did, she would go as far away from here as possible. Somehow, she willed her grandmother to understand.

ALANNA'S SCENT LINGERED in the empty cottage, the memories of their lovemaking jolting through Cain. Where had she gone? And why had she left when he'd ordered her to wait on him? Didn't she trust that he would return and help her find Simon?

Trying not to panic, he searched the rooms for a note, but came up empty. His trained gaze scanned for any sign of a struggle, any clue that someone had found Alanna and forced her to leave. But the only signs he saw were the tangled bedspread where they had made love and the wet towel she'd used earlier.

Maybe she'd taken a walk on the beach. But at midnight? He paced to the window and stared outside, looking for signs of someone combing the strip of beach behind the cottage, but a dismal blackness swallowed the night. The sound of the ocean mingling with his own rapid heartbeat roared in his ears.

Frustrated, he slumped down on the threadbare plaid sofa and dropped his head into his hands, searching the floor as if the dusty beige carpet could give him answers. Then he spotted his cell phone. His mind raced with possibilities as he jerked it up and checked for messages.

His recording played, then Luke's voice. ''Cain,

this is Luke again. Who the hell answered your phone a minute ago?"

The breath trapped in his throat.

Had Alanna answered and realized he had talked to the FBI? Sheer panic took hold of him. She didn't think he'd turn her in, did she?

The hollow emptiness in the room spoke for itself.

Hoping Luke would offer him a clue, he punched in his friend's number. Luke answered on the third ring. "Caldwell, where have you been?"

Cain relayed the mind-boggling turn of events that had ended with him finding his brother alive.

"I'm glad, man," Luke said, a note of sincerity in his voice. "But who answered your phone? Was it the Hayes woman?"

Cain hesitated. "What makes you think that?"

"Just a hunch." Irritation sharpened Luke's voice. "What's wrong with you—have you taken up your brother's calling now?"

"Let's just say I understand what drove him to do some of the things he did."

"Look, Cain, either you tell me what's going on or I'm hauling you in."

Resigned, Cain explained the story about Alanna and Simon and his suspicions.

"Geesh, no wonder you were interested in Denise Harley's research. You really think CIRP is doing research with this baby?"

"Yes, and I intend to find out what they've done with Simon." And Alanna.

And bring her back and shake her for scaring him. Then make love to her until dawn.

But then he'd have to say goodbye again. Or would he?

"You've fallen for this woman, haven't you?" Luke asked.

Even as Cain denied it, his heart clenched with worry. The past few days had been an emotional roller coaster. First thinking he'd lost Eric, then meeting Alanna and Simon and realizing they needed him. Realizing he needed them....

No, he didn't need anyone. Hadn't he learned that it was much too painful to love someone and lose them? With Eric he didn't have a choice, but with Alanna he damn well did.

"Do you think she'll try and find Simon on her own?" Luke asked.

Dear God, he hoped she didn't, but he knew her well enough by now to know she wouldn't give up without trying.

Which meant she was probably on her way back to the research center now. If they hadn't caught her already...

JUST AS ALANNA LEFT her grandmother's room, a nurse spotted her and called her name, but she ducked her head and hurried on, ignoring her. Afraid the nurse would phone the police, she rushed out the door, searching the area for Paul. She spotted him turning the corner of the building. He seemed to come out of nowhere, his face ashen, his gait slow. At least he was on his feet this time instead of in a wheelchair, but his eyes appeared glassy and his skin had a yellowish tint, the remnants of drugs, she supposed.

"Come on," he whispered, grabbing her elbow, "We have to get out of here."

"What's going on, Paul?" Alanna stopped abruptly. "I thought they were holding you."

"They were, but I sneaked out." He swayed slightly and she wondered how he'd driven there or if he'd taken a cab. "They took Simon to Nighthawk Island. We need to get to him."

She clenched his arm. "Is he all right?"

He ushered her along the sidewalk toward a gray Lexus. "I'm afraid he's not doing well."

"The blood abnormality?"

"A hoax. Peterson faked some tests to show me so I'd believe he had a liver disorder and I'd help them. But now Simon is suffering from separation anxiety."

She'd read about the condition in studies, but normally it wasn't serious.

His frown told her another story. "I guess we didn't count on the fact that with Simon's superintelligence, he'd be more sensitive to stimuli around him." He reached for the car door, looking over his shoulder. "He misses you and refuses to eat."

"That can't last," Alanna said, as much for her own comfort as his.

"Remember those studies where doctors in Europe discovered that babies didn't grow and develop because of a lack of human contact?"

"Not enough touching and cuddling, yes, I remember."

"Simon may suffer to the extreme." He laid a hand on her shoulder. "There's more, Alanna. The center has discussed bringing in Simon's father."

Alanna gripped the car door with trembling fingers. "Who is he?"

But Paul's reply was cut off when two men in dark suits suddenly appeared behind him. Alanna opened her mouth to scream and reached for the pistol in her bag, but the taller man pressed a gun to Paul's head and the other snapped her arms behind her before she could reach the gun.

CAIN PACED from one window to the other, wearing a footpath across the dusty carpet, trying to formulate a plan. Luke had offered to help and he would probably need it at some point, so he'd told him he would call. For now, he tried to think of a place Alanna might go. She'd mentioned visiting her grandmother. Or would she head straight to the research park? Surely not, not without someone to help her.

He found a scratch pad on the end table and noticed indentations where someone had written on it. Using a pencil, he shaded the page and saw the words *nursing home* had been scribbled on the pad. Of course.

It was worth a chance.

He dialed information, then asked them to patch him into the Savannah Nursing Home.

"Can you tell me if Alanna Hayes has been there to visit her grandmother tonight?"

"Who is this?" the nurse asked warily.

"A friend of hers."

"You're sure you're not the police, 'cause I don't believe for a minute that Alanna is a murderer."

He gritted his teeth. "Look, I am a friend and I'm very worried about her. Her life may be in jeopardy."

"Oh, God, she was just here a few minutes ago. I called her name so I could tell her I knew those police had made a mistake about her, but she practically ran out the door. I tried to catch her outside, but she met up with some men."

"Did you recognize the men?"

"One of them was that doctor who's been on TV talking about his missing son."

"Polenta?"

"Yes. She and the doctor were just about to get in this Lexus coupe when two men wearing fancy suits came up. Suddenly they changed their minds and Alanna and Dr. Polenta went with them."

Cain hung up, his heart in his throat. Alanna was definitely in trouble. He grabbed his keys, stuffed his phone into his jacket pocket and headed to the door.

Where would the men take her and Polenta?

Were they still alive?

Chapter Nineteen

Alanna lay on the cold floor on her side, bound and gagged, facing the door of the cruiser cabin. Paul lay a few feet away in the same condition, only still unconscious. His complexion was a pasty white, his breathing uneven. She silently willed him to wake up. They had to escape and find Simon.

The strong scent of chloroform filled her senses and she coughed, fighting to drag air into her mouth around the gag. Thankfully, the constant crash of the waves on the shore and the lack of the engine hum suggested they weren't moving. Yet.

Coupled with fear and the lingering effect of the drug, the sway of the boat made her stomach pitch to her throat. Arms numb from being tied behind her back slowly came to life with sharp pinpoints of pain as she tried to untie the ropes binding her wrists. What had Paul been on the verge of telling her about Simon's father when they'd been captured?

Fumbling futilely with the ropes, she scanned the room for something sharp to help her, but found nothing but dark shadows and the single berth and utilitarian-type furniture that comprised the suite. She should have waited for Cain, yet the memory of his betrayal splintered through her. Would he come looking for her? How would he know where to find her?

Footsteps pounded outside the door, the sound of voices spiking her heartbeat to a fever pitch.

"They know too much," a man with a deep voice said. "We'll have to kill them and dump their bodies into the ocean."

"How about the cop?"

"If he comes looking, we'll take care of him, too."

"Have you heard from Hughes?"

"He's on his way."

Alanna stiffened and pushed her feet against Paul's legs to try to wake him. They had to hurry. She couldn't let the men kill them or Cain.

"Does Hughes know about Project Simon yet?"

"I thought it'd be better if we told him in person."

A throaty chuckle followed. "Won't he be surprised to find out that not only have we resurrected the work he almost died trying to save, but from that work, he now has a son."

Alanna froze. Dear God. Arnold Hughes was Simon's father?

CAIN KNEW he needed help and agreed that Luke should fly in, but he couldn't simply sit back and wait or it might be too late. They had mulled over the possibilities of where the scientists would take Alanna and Simon. After studying the various facilities on each of the three islands, their best guess was Nighthawk Island. The remote location would provide security for them as well as the perfect spot to get rid of intruders and cover up any illegal activities.

His stomach convulsed at the thought. They might already be too late to save Alanna.

The scientists wouldn't hurt Simon, but she would be dispensable to them, as he would be if they caught him.

He didn't give a damn about himself, but he could not let her die.

The FBI already had Nighthawk Island under scrutiny so Luke had master plans of the facility's layout. Cain rented a small fishing boat, battling the wind and water spraying from the jets as he took the waves at full speed. The fifteen-minute trek seemed like hours, but he finally cut the engine and coasted into Serpent's Cove, a discreet inlet tucked on the far side of the island away from the main hub of the research facility. Stuffing his gun in the holster inside his bomber jacket, he checked for extra ammunition, smeared dirt on his face to disguise himself in the light, and crept into the shadows of the trees.

Luke had told him the island had been named after the unusual nighthawk who sometimes stole into the night to attack its prey, animal or human. He didn't miss the irony of the name and the way the legend personified the shadier side of a few of the research projects that had been uncovered.

Of course, most of the projects were legitimate, and most of the doctors truly were geniuses trying to better mankind. But there was occasionally one who either believed himself God or pushed ethics aside to use the advanced techniques for their own purpose.

The inky sky swallowed the stars, the clawlike fingers of the palms casting shadows over the land to obliterate the moon. Cain gauged his movements to keep his footsteps as soundless as possible with only an occasional snap of a twig jarring the silence. Feeling his way through the blackness of the forest by using his finely honed instincts, only a bird twittering or the slithering hiss of a snake gave him pause. Sweat beaded on his forehead as he approached the outer parameters of the main building, the sight of two security guards drawing his attention.

According to Luke's latest information, the larger concrete building housed projects, the other smaller ones nestled along the island were being renovated, one of which was being equipped with heavy decontamination equipment that had raised the eyebrows of the feds. The center claimed to be working on anti-terrorist measures, but the possibilities were endless.

Where would they take Simon and Alanna? Would they even be together?

Sneaking past the security proved difficult, but Cain finally managed by cutting through the backs of buildings, his ears and eyes tuned to see if Alanna might be in one of those. He found nothing.

A back entrance door opened, and the man who'd attacked Alanna in the graveyard exited, sliding a beefy hand over his slick bald head. Cain's gut told him the thug would lead him to Alanna. Two men wearing white lab coats stepped to the doorway, their worried gazes flickering across the trees toward the shore on the west side.

"Get it over with," the older of the two scientists

said. The beefy man nodded and a cold chill engulfed Cain. He knew exactly what the man planned to do. Kill Alanna.

He had to stop him.

Watching the hired gun push his way through the heavy bushes skirting the forest edge, Cain slunk down low and followed him to a nearby docked boat. He'd come back later for the ones who'd issued the order. He hesitated long enough to call Luke and give him his location, then crouched down and ran toward the cruiser.

Was Alanna on board? What about Simon?

ALANNA TWISTED her body, sliding it inch by inch near Paul, swinging her feet to kick his legs. He stirred and moaned, his blurry-eyed gaze working to focus on her.

She gestured frantically toward the door with a jerk of her head, then rolled so her back touched his, nodding toward her bound hands, signaling for him to untie her. It took him several seconds to focus, but his weak nod acknowledged her silent plea. Finally he rolled himself so he could untie her ropes.

The putter of the engine coming to life startled her, sending a fresh wave of panic through her. Where were they taking her?

The answer immediately came to her.

Out to sea to dump their bodies so no one could find them.

Heaven help her, why had she gone off on her own and not waited for Cain? Why hadn't she trusted him?

Because he'd lied to her and turned her in to the

feds. And after Donald's betrayal in their marriage, she hadn't been able to accept another man's lies.

But she could have left him a note and told him where to look for her in case something went wrong. She wanted to hold him in her arms one more time.

To hold Simon. He was already suffering from separation anxiety. If they killed her, would he survive without her?

The boat rocked over the crashing waves, the ominous sound of death reverberating in her ears as she pictured being tossed over the edge to the sharks. Behind her, Paul groaned and lost his grip as if he'd passed out again. She nudged him with her feet until he gathered enough energy to continue twisting at her ropes.

Simon's trusting, innocent face flashed into her head. She refused to give up. She would get free and save him. Then she'd tell Cain just what she thought about his lies.

She had come too far in her life and fought too hard for it to end like this. Simon needed her. She wasn't ready to die.

CAIN CRAWLED from beneath the tarp where he'd hidden in the storage area, wincing as the door squeaked open. The hired man steered the boat a good two miles off the shore, then dropped the anchor, leaving the helm with his gun cocked and ready to fire.

Cain waited until the man descended the three steps to the berth below, then crept behind him, his own weapon poised to fire should his footsteps give him away.

Seconds later, the door to a small cabin opened, and he heard scuffling, struggling noises. Then the man dragged Alanna outside and put the gun to her head. His heart slammed into his throat.

She had been fighting him, he could tell by the fiery gleam in her eyes and her erratic movements, but she suddenly went deathly still. Seizing her by her bound arms, he then dragged her toward the steps. Cain darted back up to the deck, crouched down and hid behind a cooler full of God knows what, holding his breath until they emerged. Ignoring the pull of his stitches, Cain attacked the man from behind.

The thug dropped Alanna's body, letting it tumble down the steps, and swung around fighting. Cain kicked his midsection, but the man pulled his gun and Cain had to fire. Shock stole the anger from the man's beefy face, and he clutched his hand to his chest as his body flew back. He collapsed against the life jackets with a grunt. Blood spurted from his chest wound and his eyes bulged.

His heart racing, Cain jumped the steps and found Alanna crumpled on the floor. When she heard his footsteps, she angled her head, eyes wide with fear.

''It's me, Alanna.''

Her terror-stricken gaze flew to his, but a quiet gasp of relief followed when she recognized him.

He pulled the sling off his arm, then knelt to untie her, drinking in the fact that she was alive. All he wanted to do was take her in his arms and kiss her, but her wary gaze held him in check. Still, he yanked the gag from her mouth and cradled her face in his hands, searching her eyes for signs of injuries. "Are you all right?"

She nodded and flicked her head toward the back cabin. "Paul—he's in there."

He untied her and helped her to stand, his stomach tightening when she ran into the cabin and dropped to her knees to rescue Polenta.

ALANNA PULLED Paul to his feet, trying to ignore the fierce relief pounding through her. Cain had saved her life. But what about Simon?

"We have to go back to the island," Cain said.

"I heard the men say Arnold Hughes is on his way," Alanna said. She turned to Paul, questions and hurt mingling together. "Is it true? Is he really Simon's father?"

Paul's face twisted in resignation. "Yes. He was the sperm donor."

"Oh, God, what are we going to do?" She glanced at Cain, panic-stricken. "He'll never give up Simon."

Alanna slid an arm around Polenta's waist. Together they staggered toward the steps to the deck. Alanna ignored the emotions playing havoc across Cain's features. Emotions that wreaked of jealousy.

She was grateful to him for saving her, but she wouldn't allow herself to fawn all over him. He had lied to her and betrayed her trust. Although she thought she'd been in love with him, Cain had never spoken of love to her.

He led the way up the steps and took over at the helm, and she breathed in the fresh salty air. While he guided the boat, Paul explained about the project.

"I hated seeing the problems families with mentally challenged children face," Paul said, regret tingeing his voice. "I had a son with terrible birth defects myself who died shortly after birth, so when Ames and Peterson first consulted me about doing experimental gene therapy on a human embryo, I thought I was doing the humanitarian thing."

"That's how you became involved in this project?"

"Yes. But Ames and Peterson worked with Hughes. They wanted to create the perfect child. I...I didn't know the sperm donor was Hughes until after you left with Simon." He bowed his head. "Even Hughes doesn't know. The doctors wanted to wait and make sure the project was successful. They didn't want Hughes to know if the therapy failed and the embryo had some terrible medical disorder or deformity."

Alanna nodded, thinking how crazy their scheme sounded. "You had noble reasons for getting involved," Alanna said softly.

Paul ran a shaky hand over a face thick with beard stubble. Cain gave her an odd look, but she dismissed it and encouraged Paul to continue. "Did the therapy work?"

"It seems to be successful, although only time will tell about Simon's intelligence. Ames and Peterson wanted to make sure Simon stayed around for observation, so they hired you to care for him."

"What about his mother?" Cain asked, a cold look in his eyes.

Paul cleared his throat, the wind howling behind

them. "That's where things really fell apart. She was a surrogate. Originally they told me she abandoned Simon. But while I was drugged, I heard them say she died in childbirth. I wondered if her death might have been related to the gene therapy but wasn't sure. There was no way to tell. They cremated her body."

"She died or they killed her?" Cain asked.

Paul frowned. "I…I really don't know. Dead or alive she would have brought unwanted attention to the center, so they covered up her existence altogether."

Alanna wiped salt water from her cheek as Cain cut the engine on the boat and let it coast into the bay on the west side. The small boat hit the rocks, then Cain threw the anchor overboard. "Did they kill the OB-GYN, too?"

"I don't know."

A security guard approached, but Cain pulled a gun and took control, ordering Polenta to tie up the guard and watch him while they went on shore to find Simon.

IRRATIONAL JEALOUSY ATE at Cain. It didn't take a fool to see that Polenta was in love with Alanna. But how did she feel about the doctor?

He had no right or claim on her, yet…. "Stay here, I'll come back for you."

"I'm going with you." Alanna stood, that fierce determination back in her eyes.

"No—"

"Cain, this is my battle. I have to."

His gaze locked with hers for a painful heartbeat

before he nodded. But not because he wanted to bow to her; he didn't want her out in the open with Polenta. She would be safer with him.

"All right, but stay behind me." He frowned. "And don't make any moves without me. Understand?"

"Yes." Her voice reeked of irritation.

"Let me go, too." Paul squared his shoulders. "I can get you through security."

"Do you have any idea where Simon is?"

He gave a clipped nod.

Cain checked the guard's bindings, and they set off, slinking through the woods until they reached the side of the main building.

"I'll get us in that back door."

Minutes later, they slipped inside and searched the halls, following Polenta through security to a lab located in the rear of the building.

Voices floated through the air ducts. Polenta steered them toward the sound, freezing occasionally to hide from another security guard. Although, given the time of night, the place was virtually empty, making it easier to find the lab. Polenta opened the door, but Cain pushed him behind him, along with Alanna. Cain wielded his gun and faced down the two scientists.

"We've been expecting you," the gray-haired man said.

Polenta appeared beside him. "It's over, Ames. Give it up."

Both men's startled gazes flooded with anger. "I

thought you were dead,'' the other man, obviously Peterson, growled.

''How many people are you going to kill to keep your project a secret?'' Cain asked.

Ames raised a pistol. ''As many as it takes.''

Cain shoved Polenta and Alanna out of the way just as the man fired.

Chapter Twenty

Alanna fell backward against Paul, the two of them flying into the hallway wall as gunfire rippled through the room. Paul threw his arms over her, and they huddled heads down on the floor in the corner. Suddenly a loud rumbling thundered above, nearly drowning out the pelting bullets. A helicopter had flown over the building and was landing somewhere very close.

Then quiet descended as quickly as the chaos had burst out.

A quiet that sent a chill up her spine. Cain? Had he been shot?

Her pulse racing, she pushed away from Paul. But just as she started toward the door again, Cain walked into the entry, his expression grave, his head downcast. "Ames and Peterson are dead." Then she spotted the squirming bundle in his arm and her heart leaped with joy.

"Simon."

"Mama," Simon whimpered. "Miss you."

Tears welled in Alanna's eyes. "I missed you too, darling."

Cain strode toward her, crooning comforting sounds to the baby. Alanna's legs wobbled as she gently eased Simon into her arms. Her gaze met with Cain's, the aching hunger in his eyes mirroring her own. Then he kissed Simon gently on the forehead and released him. Considering the violence that had just transpired, the gesture was so oddly tender and intimate that her heart clenched again.

Cain was an honorable man.

And Alanna loved him.

But what could come of that love?

"I knew they wouldn't give it up," Paul said. "They both let their egos and greed take over and lost all sense of morality."

A security guard rushed toward them with two suited men on his tail. Cain met them halfway, identifying himself. "Thanks, Luke, but it's over."

Luke? The man from the FBI. Alanna's arms trembled as she hugged Simon to her. Were they going to arrest her now and take Simon away from her again?

A HELICOPTER RIDE LATER, Cain sat with Alanna and Polenta in an interrogation room at the FBI headquarters in Atlanta. Luke and another agent had drilled them relentlessly on each of their actions, sorting through Polenta's story with a fine-tooth comb, taking notes on all aspects of the research center and its work for further scrutiny.

"Were there any doctors involved in the project other than Ames and Peterson?"

"The OB-GYN was the only one I know of."

"Did Peterson and Ames have him killed?"

"I don't think so," Polenta said. "But I can't be

certain. They kept me drugged a good bit of the time the past couple of weeks.''

Luke leaned his hands on the scarred table in front of Polenta and glared into his eyes. ''Do you know where Arnold Hughes is now?''

''No.'' Polenta showed his first onslaught of nerves. ''Believe me, if he knew Simon was his baby, he'd already have been here.''

''But you know for certain he's alive?''

''That's what I heard. He had plastic surgery but I have no idea what he looks like now.'' Paul paused. ''But he doesn't know Simon is his son.''

''Did he have anything to do with bombing my brother's car?'' Cain asked.

Polenta shrugged, his voice contrite. ''I can't be sure. Ames gave me a truth serum after Alanna disappeared, so I could have given them Eric's name. I'm sorry.''

''I am, too, Cain,'' Alanna said softly.

''At least he's alive,'' Cain said, realizing they hadn't had a chance to talk since he'd seen Eric. Then he'd come back for her and found the empty house....

Simon began to fuss and Alanna jiggled him in her arms to soothe him.

''What about the baby's mother?'' Luke asked.

''I believe she's dead.''

''Did you find out anything about that reporter?'' Alanna asked.

Cain turned to Luke, but he shook his head. ''Phyllis French worked for the paper, but they gave her medical leave a few months ago. She had a miscarriage and hasn't been stable since. We're still looking for her for questioning.''

"What if she knows about Hughes?"

Cain rubbed Alanna's back to comfort her. "We'll locate her and find out exactly what she does know." Simon gurgled and Cain reached out and let the baby grab his thumb.

"I want to adopt Simon," Alanna said, tucking the blanket around Simon's feet.

Tension thrummed between them as her hand brushed over Simon. Simon and Alanna were safe for now, but how long would it be before Hughes came looking for them?

Cain cleared his throat. "Luke, I think we should get Alanna and Simon into the witness protection program, give them new identities. You know Hughes will look for the baby once he finds out about him."

Luke's eyebrows climbed his forehead. "We could use them as bait to catch Hughes."

A fist slammed into Cain's gut. "Absolutely not."

Alanna's panicked gaze flew to Cain's.

"Listen, Caldwell, it's the best plan—"

"I said no." Cain glared at Luke. "They've been through enough. There's no way I'd let you put either one of them in danger again." He ignored Luke's questioning look. "We'll have to find another way to trap Hughes."

"Eventually he's going to learn that the baby is his and come after them," Luke said.

Polenta stood, dark brows furrowed. "Not if I destroy any evidence that Simon belongs to him."

Hope glittered in Alanna's eyes. "You would really do that, Paul?"

Polenta turned to Alanna and Simon and lifted a

hand to her cheek, a gesture that sent Cain's temper
into a roar.

"Of course, Alanna. There hasn't been a day since
I got involved with this project that I haven't regretted
it. My family at home would be ashamed of my actions, as am I."

Without realizing what he was doing, Cain moved
to Alanna's side.

Anxiety knotted the muscles in his neck at her softening expression. Just exactly how did she feel about
Polenta? If Cain couldn't offer her love and commitment, would she turn to the doctor?

THE NEXT FEW HOURS FLEW BY in a whirlwind of ac-
tivity as the federal agents worked to secure Alanna
and Simon a new place to live. Though filled with
relief to have Simon in her arms and the hopes of a
new future, Alanna battled an inner war of emotions.
Cain's friend had assured her that once she and Simon
were settled, they would move her grandmother to a
new nursing home, and place her under a different
name. Alanna could visit her regularly. Only Luke
and Cain would know Alanna's whereabouts, and
they had devised a special code so she could phone
one of them if necessary. Another agent had escorted
Paul back to the lab to destroy any evidence that
might link Simon to Arnold Hughes, then they took
him to the hotel.

The short ride to the hotel where Alanna would
stay was filled with tension. Finally Alanna could
stand the excruciating silence no longer.

"Thank you for all that you've done for me and

Simon,'' she said, after settling Simon into bed for the night.

Cain stood in the doorway between the suite area and bedroom, as if he didn't know whether to come all the way inside or leave completely. Alanna's heart squeezed as she realized he would choose the latter.

His job, his brother, his life, all the things that mattered to him were in Atlanta.

Their situation had brought them together, but now it would tear them apart. Or maybe it was the fact that Cain didn't love her that would take him away from her.

An ache, soul deep, opened up inside her. But she refused to beg him to stay or guilt him into loving her when she'd caused him so much trouble already.

She loved him too much to do anything so devious.

''I'm glad that it all worked out.'' His gruff voice sent need pulsing through her. She remembered the husky sound of his lovemaking, the torturous way his fingers had teased her into bliss, the way her body had burned with heat at his possession.

''Why did you leave the beach cottage?'' Cain's gaze bored into hers.

''You promised you wouldn't tell the FBI, then your friend called…''

Disappointment flitted across his features. ''We were in over our heads, Alanna. Even I had to admit I needed help.''

She swallowed, his words hitting home. But could she admit she needed him? Did he want her to? She wasn't sure.

''I'm really glad you get to keep Simon.''

Tears filled her eyes. ''I do love him, Cain. I…I

never thought it would work out for me to keep him forever. I owe you.''

''You don't owe me anything. I was just doing my job.'' In spite of his declaration, emotions clouded his dark eyes. ''I'd like for Eric to see Simon someday.''

Another reason he had to leave. His brother had been hurt terribly because of her. And Eric still had a long recovery ahead. Surgeries. Skin grafts. Therapy.

How could Cain not blame her for his brother's suffering?

''I...I guess I should go. I know you're exhausted.''

She ached to stop him from walking out, but she remained frozen in her spot. ''And I know you want to see Eric.''

''He's going to need me now,'' Cain said in a low voice. His gaze dropped to Simon on the bed and lingered. Then he walked toward the bed and brushed a kiss across the baby's forehead. Slowly he straightened and his dark eyes met hers. Tears blurred her vision as he wrapped his uninjured arm around her, then pulled her against him and kissed her. His lips moved gently first, then with such hunger that her legs buckled. Simon cooed, bringing them both back to reality.

She was breathless and trembling with unsated hunger when he turned to leave, but she managed to lock the door behind him. Then she stood with her forehead pressed against the closed door and listened until his footsteps completely faded, her heart splintering into a thousand pieces.

Thankfully Cain had brought the baby back to her.

She only wished…wished for what? It had been forever since she'd allowed herself to need someone.

But in the darkness of the night she silently admitted that she needed Cain.

Only she didn't think he'd wanted to hear it.

EMOTIONS WARRED within Cain all the way to the hospital. Eric needed him, but Alanna no longer did; why did that fact bother him so? He admired her independence, respected her for standing on her own, for not clinging to him and begging him to stay. She'd given him permission to return to his job, to his responsibilities, to his brother. He didn't like scenes, didn't want emotional attachments. God knows he remembered the pain of losing his mother, the grief he'd felt when he'd stood at that graveyard in the dismal rain, thinking he'd buried his brother.

Then Alanna had appeared with Simon, adding to his turmoil and things had spiraled out of control. He had crossed the line with her on this case, delved into grays that he'd sworn to avoid all his life. Getting involved with a suspect or victim under his care had never been an option, much less something he'd allowed to happen. His anguished state had altered his judgment; the fear had altered hers. There was no other logical explanation for the fact that he'd let her get under his skin.

He never should have slept with her.

He was glad the case was over, that he could get on with his life.

Wasn't he?

And then there was Simon, that precious little boy…

His mind spinning with questions, he entered the ICU, and was surprised to find Eric had been moved to a room.

"He's doing much better," the head ICU nurse said.

She gave him the room number and he took the elevator, contemplating the hard haul his brother had ahead of him.

"Hey, man," Eric said in voice still hoarse from the respirator.

"You're looking better." Not that he could see much beyond the bandages, but Eric was sitting up. That had to be a good sign.

"I'll be better when I get out of this damn place."

Cain chuckled and moved to the edge of Eric's bed. "How are you doing, bro?"

Eric shrugged, his tough-boy act in place. "All right. Hurts like hell, but they're keeping me pretty doped up." He raised his hand, touched his fingers to the bandage on his cheek. "I don't imagine I'm going to look very good."

Cain had to swallow twice before he could talk. "You look better than you did in that casket."

That brought Eric's hand away. "I hate that the guy died…"

"It's not your fault. We think Arnold Hughes is responsible."

"He's the man who wanted Alanna and the baby?"

"Yeah." Cain filled him in on everything that had happened.

"So, she's going to get to adopt the baby?"

"Yeah, and this time the feds did their job. They're going to help her relocate."

Eric wrestled with the sheet, pulling it over his bandaged thigh. Cain thought of all the times they'd argued, how much he'd regretted the disagreement they'd had that last day.

Of how he'd wished he'd told his brother how much he admired him.

He couldn't wait any longer. Taking the vinyl chair beside the bed, he bowed his head. "Eric, I can't tell you how I felt when I thought you were gone. I hated that we'd fought—"

"You don't have to do this," Eric said, his own voice uncharacteristically full of emotion.

"Yes, I do." Cain met his gaze head-on. "I never understood how you saw things before, and we may not always see things eye-to-eye in the future, but I understand the grays now." He emitted a self-deprecating chuckle. "There are lots of grays." He cleared his throat. "I admire you for all the people you helped along the way."

"Found yourself in that murky water with Alanna, huh?"

His brother must have read more than he'd intended in Cain's voice. Instead of arguing though, he nodded.

"What exactly happened between the two of you?"

"Nothing."

"Don't lie to me, Cain. I can see it in your eyes every time you say her name."

"Maybe." He shrugged, battling emotions he didn't care to feel. Like want and need and...and love? "But nothing can come of it. I'm a cop, I don't have room for anyone in my life."

"'Cause you're afraid of losing them again?"

Cain raised his head. Seconds earlier, he'd admitted to his brother how hard it had been when he'd thought Eric was dead. And when his mother had died, he'd been so busy taking care of Eric he hadn't dwelled on his own pain, his own sense of desertion…

Had he let that subconscious fear of being deserted again, of losing someone, keep him from falling in love?

"You care about this woman, don't you?"

"I…" He started to deny it, but the words lodged in his windpipe.

"You're crazy if you let her go and don't tell her."

Cain steepled his hands in front of him. Eric was right. When he thought he'd lost Eric, he'd regretted not telling him how he felt.

He couldn't let Alanna go without telling her that he loved her.

EXHAUSTION PINCHED Alanna's shoulder muscles as she dressed in a nightgown and robe, but she knew sleep would not come quickly. Every moment she'd been in Cain's arms haunted her, the feeling of loneliness that had engulfed her when he'd driven away growing more intense with every minute. Reminding herself she should be grateful to be safe, to have Simon in her life forever, she tried to banish the memories of Cain from her mind.

Because occasionally daydreams of marriage and raising Simon with Cain flashed into her head. Hadn't she learned that dreams didn't come true? That love was foolish, a waste of time and energy?

Frustrated, she paced the confines of the hotel suite,

irritated that the shadows from the corners and noises outside the door still startled her.

A soft knock penetrated the haze around her, and she stumbled toward the door. Cain and Luke were the only two people who knew her location. Had Cain returned to see her?

To tell her that he couldn't live without her, that he loved her?

Butterflies fluttered in her chest as she clutched the knob. "Who is it?"

"It's Phyllis French, Ms. Hayes. Please let me come in."

"What are you doing here?" Adrenaline shot through Alanna. "How…how did you find me?"

"Look, Ms. Hayes, it doesn't matter, but you have to see me. It's about Simon, and it's important."

Alanna gulped. Maybe she should call Cain or Luke—

"I have Simon's birth certificate, Ms. Hayes. I know who his mother is."

"His mother is dead," Alanna said through the door.

"No, she isn't. She's very much alive and I can prove it."

Chapter Twenty-One

Cain raced toward Alanna's hotel, anxious to confess to her that he loved her. It had taken a damn long time for him to admit it to himself.

He only hoped she returned his feelings.

Blood pulsed through his veins in a rapid staccato rhythm as he approached the hotel. Hunger unlike anything he'd ever known drove him. For a man who hadn't wanted love, he certainly felt desperate to have her fall into his arms. Then he would strip off her clothes, touch every inch of her sweet body until she cried out his name and begged him never to leave.

His cell phone rang just as he pulled in the parking lot.

"Caldwell here."

"It's Paul Polenta."

Cain gulped. "What is it, Polenta?"

"You have to get to Alanna. That French woman. She's deranged. She came to my hotel room here looking for Simon."

"What?"

"She shot me—"

"Are you all right?"

"Don't worry about me. The paramedics are on their way. You have to save Alanna. The woman claims Simon is her baby."

Wind slapped Cain's face as he jumped from his car, ice freezing in his veins. "How did she find you?" He checked his weapon as he ran across the parking lot and into the hotel.

"She said she'd followed me to my hotel. She's searching the rooms now for Alanna."

Dammit, they should have put the two of them in different hotels for the night.

"I'm almost there." Cain took the inside stairs two at a time. "Hughes hasn't shown up, has he?"

"No, I destroyed all references to Project Simon and his birth. Hughes will never know he has a son. But there's something else," Polenta said breathlessly. "I was wrong about Simon's mother being dead. I found the original files on the project. You aren't going to believe who Simon's mother really is."

Cain halted at the door, stunned at Polenta's next words. But he reached Alanna's room and alarm shot through him at the sound of the women's heated voices inside.

ALANNA HADN'T MEANT to let Phyllis French inside the room, but she'd opened the door barely enough for the woman to slip the papers about Simon's mother through and the woman had busted the chain lock on the door.

Now Phyllis's hand trembled as she pointed a small pistol at Alanna's chest.

"You're Simon's real mother?" Alanna went numb with shock. "Paul said she died."

"They lied to you just like they did to me." Agitation lined Phyllis's hard features. "I went to the fertility clinic to have in vitro and it worked, but I had a miscarriage at six months. Then I learned I had another child. The egg they fertilized to make Simon, it was my egg."

This couldn't be happening. Just when Alanna thought Simon was hers forever. "How can you be sure?"

"I know Simon is mine." Phyllis waved the gun toward the piece of paper. Instead of a birth certificate, she held a computer printout from the lab at Nighthawk Island showing the details of Project Simon, the source of sperm and egg donors.

Alanna's eyes blurred with tears when she saw Phyllis French's name printed on the sheet listing her as an egg donor.

"They used my egg and gave it to someone else, a surrogate mother," Phyllis said, her voice gaining in momentum. "Then they killed that woman and hired you to take care of my baby boy. I want him now."

Alanna glanced at the bedroom door, her heart aching. She had to stall. She couldn't let this woman leave with Simon. "I have temporary custody now. We'll have to go to the authorities, have DNA testing—"

"No, I've waited long enough. I'm prepared to go to the press with the story," Phyllis assured her. "So don't even think about having your boyfriend cover up the DNA tests to keep me from getting Simon."

"I wouldn't do such a thing." Alanna struggled to keep her talking, to give herself time to think. "You knew about Project Simon from the beginning?"

"No, after I had a miscarriage. I was devastated, but then I found out they'd kept one of my eggs." Her eyes blazed with anger. "I'm not leaving without my Simon."

The woman took a step forward, the gun bobbing up and down with her shaky hand. Alanna froze. But suddenly the door swung open and Cain stepped inside, his own weapon drawn by his side.

"Put the gun down, Ms. French. You're not Simon's mother."

Phyllis whirled around, swinging the gun toward Cain. "Yes, I am!"

"No." Cain stalked forward, fury in his eyes. "I just talked to Polenta, right after you shot him and left him to die. He discovered the truth about an hour ago."

"What?" Alanna gasped.

"Ms. French had the research papers altered so she could claim Simon. She killed the OB-GYN so he couldn't reveal the truth."

"Simon's mother is dead?" Alanna asked.

"Simon is mine!" Phyllis roared.

The blood thundered in Alanna's ears as Phyllis fired the first shot. Cain leaped forward and tried to grab the gun. They struggled wildly, falling to the floor in a tangle of arms and legs. Alanna jumped into action to help, but the gun went off again and a grunt of pain followed.

Cain raised up slowly, his expression clouded with sorrow. Phyllis French had just died.

Alanna dropped down to see if Cain was all right. "Are you hurt?"

"No." He yanked her into his arms, drew her to her feet and ushered them to the corner of the room, far away from the cruel reality of the French woman's death. "God, I was scared to death when I saw her with that gun." He searched her face, then cupped her cheeks in his hands and kissed her. "I don't know what I would have done if something had happened to you."

"Cain, shh, I'm okay."

His mouth descended on hers, claiming her with a kiss that was both erotic and tender. His possession rang loud and clear. "I love you, Alanna. I really love you. Please don't ever leave me."

Cain held his breath, afraid Alanna would confess her love for Polenta. Afraid he'd finally given his heart but that she might crush it by turning him away.

Tears filled Alanna's eyes, her heart melting. "I love you, too, Cain. I'll never leave you. Never."

He pressed his lips to hers in a mind-numbing kiss. Seconds later, their heated embrace was broken by a baby's babble.

Alanna pulled back, her breathing raspy. "Cain, I have to know. Was that woman Simon's mother?"

"No." Cain cupped her face in his hands. "You are, Alanna." He whispered another kiss into her hair. "Simon is your son."

HOURS LATER, after the police and federal agents had left and Phyllis French's body had been removed, Cain lay in bed with Alanna.

Desire still burned through him. They had already

made love twice, but he still hadn't slaked his hunger for her. He would never get enough of touching her, kissing and licking her body, hearing her cry out his name in ecstasy.

Alanna rolled over and curled into his arms, one finger trailing down his bare chest, sending a quiver through his body. The shadow of blond hair shone through the black roots of her hair, reminding him of how she'd come to him in disguise. How she'd broken down the walls around him a little bit at a time with her courage and loving care and that innocent child.

He pressed his lips to her forehead and held her tight. "Now that we know all the players in Project Simon and that you are really Simon's mother, I don't think you'll need to stay undercover."

"What about Hughes?"

"Polenta said he's already destroyed any evidence linking the experiment to Hughes. He'll never know he's Simon's father."

"Thank God." She curled a hand over his stomach. "All I want is for Simon to have as normal a life as possible."

"And we'll give it to him." He tilted her chin up. "You know it will be safer if you cut any ties with Polenta. Can you do that?"

"Yes." She traced a finger over his mouth. "Paul was a friend, Cain. Nothing more."

He gripped her hand in his and kissed her fingers gently, the relief in his sigh audible.

"I never expected to find out I was his mother. Or to fall in love with you." She pressed a kiss to his mouth.

"Marry me, Alanna."

She bit down on her lower lip. "I'm not sure we should get married."

His breath caught in his throat. "What?" He cupped her chin in his hands so he could stare into her eyes, nerves bunching his stomach. Did the idea of being married to a cop frighten her too much? Was she afraid for Simon to grow up with the dangers of his job constantly in their lives? "Is it my job—"

"No. Your job is part of you." She pressed a finger to his lip. "It's …it's me. I may not be able to conceive another child. That is…if you want more children."

A heartbeat of strained silence yawned between them before Cain leaned forward and nibbled at her mouth. "All I want is you, Alanna. Don't you know that? I just want you…"

Cain rose above her.

He smiled and lowered himself over her and kissed her tenderly. "And Simon." His husky voice resonated with passion and promises. "The little boy who brought us together."

* * * * *

Be sure to pick up Rita Herron's next books in the Hartwell Hope Chest *series,*
HAVE BOUQUET, NEED BOYFRIEND
and HAVE COWBOY, NEED CUPID.
Coming in June and July 2003 from
Harlequin American Romance.

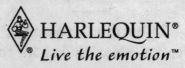

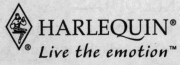

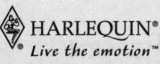

This summer
New York Times bestselling author

HEATHER GRAHAM

&

Golden Heart Award Winner

JULIA JUSTISS

come together in

Forbidden Stranger

(on sale June 2003)

**Don't miss this
captivating 2-in-1
collection brimming
with the intoxicating
allure of forbidden love!**

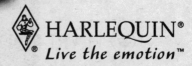

◆ HARLEQUIN®
Live the emotion™

Visit us at www.eHarlequin.com

PHFS

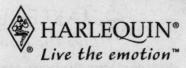

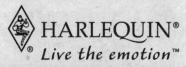

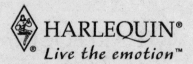